LITTLE MISS EVIL

LITTLE MISS EVIL

A NICK HOFFMAN MYSTERY

Lev Raphael

Walker & Company New York

First published in the United States of America in 2000 by
Walker Publishing Company, Inc.

Published simultaneously in Canada by Fitzhenry and Whiteside,
Markham, Ontario L3R 4T8

Library of Congress Cataloging-in-Publication Data
Raphael, Lev.
Little Miss Evil: a Nick Hoffman mystery   /   Lev Raphael.
p. cm.
ISBN 0-8027-3342-5
1. Hoffman, Nick (Fictitious character)—Fiction. 2. College
teachers—Michigan—Fiction. 3. Michigan—Fiction. I. Title.
PS3568.A5988 L56 2000
813'.54—dc21   99-088139

Series design by Mary Jane DiMassi

Printed in the United States of America
2 4 6 8 10 9 7 5 3 1

in memory of my mother
Lalka Klackzo
who inspired my love of mysteries

It is the bright day that brings forth the adder
And that craves wary walking.

1

D O you think we spend too much time on food?" I asked. Stefan turned from the cutting board where he had just finished dicing leeks and shallots for a potato lasagna with wild mushrooms and a celery herb sauce. He frowned. "What do you mean?"

I put down the glass of Délixir de Noix, the delicious walnut aperitif my cousin Sharon had sent us as a souvenir from her recent trip to the Dordogne, where walnut oil and walnuts were so integral a part of the cuisine that there was even a walnut museum. Or so she claimed.

"Well, we talk about it, we read food magazines, restaurant reviews, sometimes even plan vacations around where we're going to eat. Think about how we do Stratford." We went to that Ontario town's renowned Shakespeare festival every summer and always ate at its best and most expensive restaurant, The Church. "And just look at all this—!" I waved around the kitchen we'd had remodeled over the summer with gray-blue granite countertops and backsplashes; antiqued, glass-doored cabinetry; and appliance garages that reduced the clutter.

"Are you saying you're sorry we changed the kitchen?"

"No—that's not my point." I jabbed an Émile Zola finger at our three shelves of cookbooks and wine books, alphabetized by country (the former) and region (the latter). Our favorites in each category were frayed and stained. "Look at all that stuff!"

"Okay." Stefan nodded, the knife in his hand motionless. Stefan occasionally preferred knives over the Cuisinart, whose noise he found distracting. "And?"

"Well, maybe we should eat more simply."

To celebrate the fading of summer, and to steel ourselves for the beginning of the State University of Michigan's fall semester which cruelly started before Labor Day, we were making a leisurely dinner course by course that Sunday night before the first week of classes. A half hour ago, we had begun with chilled Cavaillon melon halves filled with port, sitting on comfortable bar stools at the new granite-topped kitchen island.

"Eat more simply—" Stefan repeated, glancing around us as if he were a king surveying his palace before fleeing the gunfire of a military coup. Then he smiled, and I could tell I was going to feel busted. Like many long-standing couples, Stefan and I didn't so much read each other's minds as read between the lines of what the other one was saying (sometimes there was a little subtext, sometimes there was a whole opera).

"Nick, you've been reading too many of those Janet Evanovich books," he said.

I had to grin. "Got it in one."

Stefan had been sampling the books I was considering teaching in my upcoming course in mystery fiction at the State University of Michigan, and he had some definite opinions of his own. Comic mysteries just weren't his thing.

He said, "You need to straighten yourself out—read some Dennis Lehane."

"That could work."

"And if I ever come home and find you eating peanut butter out of a jar or chomping down on cold pizza or handfuls of corn flakes, I'm not going to think you're simplifying your life, I'm going to assume you've got a new kind of Alzheimer's."

I was indeed experiencing a Stephanie Plum overdose, or side effect. Enjoying Evanovich's first few light mysteries, I'd been struck by how different hapless Stephanie's eating habits were from mine, and I was oddly, perhaps morbidly, fascinated. That drew me along in her series as much as the comic misadventures. It wasn't that I wanted her life (and in New Jersey!), but it intrigued me that she was so lackadaisical about food unless her mother was cooking. I wondered what it would feel like, and was almost a little ashamed of our devotion to eating well.

Stefan said, "Cooking isn't something I ever want to simplify. I need to spend time in the kitchen just like I need to spend time at the gym. It helps me relax."

That was unassailable. Stefan had to be able to unhook from obsessing about his fading career as a novelist. He may have started out well, over a decade ago, in a welter of good reviews, but literary fiction was as enticing a prospect these days as a Robert Mapplethorpe retrospective to Jesse Helms. General sales were "trending down," as his agent put it, and Stefan's were leading the way. He had, in fact, reached the low point of his career.

Stefan's agent had been unable to sell his latest novel after his longtime publisher (which had been bought by a German conglomerate) dropped him from its list; his previous book hadn't gone into paperback; and his sales had been so weak that his last book was remaindered within a year of publication—a dismal first for him.

He'd been so upset about the book's failure that when a late review came in from the tiny *Gaylord Gazette* up in northern Michigan, he'd exploded at its many factual inaccuracies—and worse. "This reviewer named Una Vole—can you believe that name?—criticizes my style, says that 'access of affection' is wrong. It's not wrong. It means *onrush* or *surge*."

I remembered having proofread the novel, as I always did with his books, and suggested those last two choices precisely because less well-read people might think the word was a typo for *excess*. But Stefan had refused, insisting the rhythm of the sentence would change. Stefan had written a witty, angry, insulting letter to the reviewer, which I read on his computer screen and suggested he delete, using a line I'd used before: "Do you want to be known as a fine writer or a maniac?" He wavered, and I added, "You'll piss this nobody little reviewer off by pointing out her mistake, so what will it get you?" He backed off, muttering, and I felt relieved to have saved him from embarrassing himself.

"I love cooking. I need to relax," Stefan said in the kitchen, turning away and wielding the knife with savage efficiency. I didn't have trouble imagining who he might be picturing under the blade.

Aggravating Stefan's profound sense of shame over his career slide was the very disturbing presence of a brand-new member of the department: Pulitzer Prize–winning novelist Camille Cypriani, whom one critic called "a cross between Anita Brookner and Judith Krantz" for her literate but sexy best-sellers about lonely women in Paris and other glamorous cities. Over the summer, sixtyish Cypriani, who had been living in Boston, had been given a newly created endowed chair of women's literature in the English, American Studies, and Rhetoric Department (EAR) at the kind of salary only administrators make: $175,000.

Her surprise entrance into the department had thrust Stefan from his position as the most important writer—not that it had meant much lately. EAR's writing program was in chaos because two of its stalwarts, the husband-and-wife team Auburn and Mavis Kinderhoek, had been mostly either sick or on leave in the years we'd been at SUM. They were bitter and combative, so that was good for Stefan, but bad for students who couldn't depend on getting the writing workshops they wanted, when they wanted.

As the foremost Edith Wharton bibliographer, I would never face the same kind of pressure Stefan was under. The Olympians in the tiny field of Wharton studies, Cynthia Griffin Wolff and R. W. B. Lewis, were charming and supportive, but even if they hadn't been, no one could really supplant me because my work was invaluable and significant.

In addition to the summer timing, there were other anomalies about Camille's position. Her endowment was anonymous and surprising in its specifications. For her first year, Cypriani didn't even have to teach or work with students; all she was required to do was host an occasional "literary luncheon" with writing students and faculty, and do one reading for the public. The whole situation was humiliating for Stefan because he wasn't consulted about the choice—everything connected to the position went through the provost's office. And Stefan not only felt dwarfed by Cypriani's reputation and her salary, but she had snubbed him in the past and continued to do so whenever they happened to meet on campus or in town.

I watched Stefan work. He looked a lot like Ben Cross in *Chariots of Fire*, only shorter and more muscular, and right now he could have been one of that rash of new-wave hunky chefs displaying his good looks on the cover of a cookbook, laying himself out like a buffet.

"You like cooking and eating, too," he said quietly. "You even like the grocery shopping. It makes sense. It's soothing. How else could you deal with working in a department of psychopaths?"

"I've never called them that."

"You've called them everything *but*."

"Fair enough."

"Is sociopaths better?"

"Maybe." More accurately, though, you could describe my colleagues in EAR as *The Planet of the Apes* on a really bad hair day. And every year there I seemed to be living through another cheesy sequel.

People tell you that academia isn't the real world, but what could be more real than envy, hypocrisy, back-stabbing, overblown rhetoric, cruelty, obsession with reputation, and the steady shredding of other people's dignity? The only things missing are real weapons and real money—but you wouldn't know that from the ferocity of faculty squabbles.

Unaware of this cross between Chernobyl and *Chinatown* before getting my Ph.D., I had become one of its denizens because I loved teaching—but heading into my fifth year at the

State University of Michigan in Michiganapolis (SUM), I wondered if I'd make it through another five after this one, even if I *were* to get tenure. Stefan had it already and was set for life in a position that was prestigious—writer-in-residence—even if out in the publishing world his name had turned to bookstore poison. I, on the other hand, was a composition professor. That made me in the academic world only a lost figure in the great army of academics and just a step or two above temporary instructors and graduate assistants—disposable, replaceable, hardly worth anyone's notice.

Let's put it this way: if composition professors had been the ones holding off the Persians, nobody would ever have heard of Thermopylae.

Ironically, though, given our interests, Stefan had become less successful since we had moved to Michiganapolis from western Massachusetts and from a series of temporary positions, and in a way you could say that I'd become more so. I was one of the most popular professors at the State University of Michigan in Michiganapolis, but for all the wrong reasons: scandal and murder.

Three years of murder, in fact. First my office mate, then people at an Edith Wharton conference I'd organized, and later students I'd known. While my record of murdered acquaintances wasn't as bad as Jessica Fletcher's, it was still deeply troubling to me. This notoriety was not exactly the way I'd hoped to make my mark. I was, after all, a bibliographer, and what could be further from that kind of dogged, scrupulous, nitpicky research than murder? Postal workers, victims of horrific abuse, and followers of racist creeds might go berserk, but when's the last time you heard a reporter talk about index cards and photocopying in the context of serial killing?

And even though my background did help prepare me for trying to figure out what was going on in each instance, nobody in my department seemed to appreciate the connection between bibliography and sleuthing—or give me points for my investigations. Like someone in a witness protection program, our university prized order and normality over everything else. So my colleagues, my department chair, and the SUM administration squirmed because I'd been involved in so much bad publicity for the university.

But SUM students were loving it.

After my third "episode" the previous spring semester, students had started crowding my regular office hours, clamoring for appointments when they couldn't make those, and just showing up at odd times in the hope of seeing me. It doesn't sound dramatic to anyone who hasn't been a teacher at the college level. But the truth is that except for sycophants, students typically avoid office hours for fear of saying something stupid to their professors—with no place to hide!—or because they dislike the class and can't bear any extra exposure to its "content provider," as professors were supposed to be called according to some idiotic new university decree.

This flow of students to my office was matched by the students signing up for my classes, each of which had been overenrolled in preregistration, leaving me in the unpleasant and unusual position of having to tell students they couldn't add me to their schedules. The mystery class I was scheduled to teach the following spring semester had been filled to capacity within minutes of opening for registration, and EAR had received a stream of complaints from students demanding that I teach another section.

Even before the semester had started, the students surged expectantly to my new office in crumbling Parker Hall as if it were a tiny theme park: Murder World. And, frankly, my own brush with death and all the wild stories about me in Michigan and national media guaranteed that I could have cleaned up if I'd opened a souvenir stand, or at least sold a few postcards and snow globes.

I mused over all this during our quiet dinner as we poured glass after glass of Bergerac Sec in the kitchen, listening to Cesaria Evora's soulful *Miss Perfumado* album and mourning the coming change in the rhythm of our days. Were we spoiled by having the summer off from teaching? Yes, and most people worked harder jobs, though I doubt that anyone but other academics had such bizarre colleagues, which balanced it all out.

The windows were open on a surprisingly cool August evening, and we could hear the hissing of summer lawns, kids riding bikes, and the harmless hum of a postwar neighborhood of tree-lined streets and unostentatious well-landscaped homes north of SUM's sprawling, verdant campus.

After the lasagna, Stefan and I took half a pot of Kona, along with a plate of hazelnut cream cheese brownies, out to the sun room and watched the sky stripe itself in blue and black. Biting into my second brownie, I thought that Stephanie Plum had no idea what she was missing.

But while I was feeling replete, Stefan clearly wasn't thinking about our wonderful meal anymore. The magic and focus of preparation, the whole Zen way he had of cooking and serving, had evaporated. I could tell by the supernally quiet way he sat looking out at the backyard, where the gazebo seemed to glow as darkness poured down around it. When you live with an introvert, you get to realize there are many kinds of silences.

"Camille," I said.

He nodded. "Camille."

I may have admired her writing somewhat (not that I would dare tell Stefan), but in just a few chance meetings, I'd come to loathe Camille for the contemptuous way she treated Stefan and almost everyone else she had contact with. She had instantly become the most powerful member of the department, enjoyed showing it off, and even had the office to do it in. I suppose only in academia can somebody's office assignment become so controversial—and the semester hadn't even started.

The neglected—but at least nominally honored—Grace Jurevicius Memorial Library on Parker Hall's second floor had been dismantled and turned into Cypriani's office. This library had for twenty years housed the extensive collection of criticism, American fiction, and Michigania willed to EAR by a beloved and benign former chair from a less contentious era at SUM. It had been disbanded, the sign removed, and the books boxed and supposedly sent off to SUM's Special Collections in clear violation of both Jurevicius's will and department tradition. This was reason enough for most EAR faculty to resent Cypriani: not only was her office huge and blessed with a gorgeous view of SUM's old central campus, but almost everyone in EAR felt that she and her adherents had committed an act of desecration. I'd never met Grace Jurevicius, but it struck even me as ugly and insensitive. And typical.

"So what's next?" I'd asked in the EAR main office. "Burning all the books from the Jurevicius Library at Homecoming?" The line shot through the department as quickly as a fake political rumor on the Internet, and faculty members who had still barely noticed me even after four years stopped me to tell me they applauded my stand. I hadn't made a stand, just a joke, but in the superheated atmosphere of Parker Hall, who knew the difference?

I'd been especially praised by tiny Iris Bell and that cipher Carter Savery, two of the many downtrodden professors in EAR, who made a habit of outrage and were so incensed at Cypriani's hiring that they'd broadcast threats about filing a grievance. These sansculottes—who were on my tenure review committee—were former members of the old Rhetoric Department, which had been abolished well over a decade ago. Its quarrelsome and underqualified faculty had been amalgamated with English and American Studies, creating a bifurcated department whose split had never been healed. They were stuck teaching the EAR faculty's least popular course, composition, and because of departmental prejudice, their own abrasive personalities, and a generally poor publishing record, they were at the bottom of their rank in salary.

But however unlikable, they were going to judge my tenure application, and I had bragged to Stefan about their praise of me.

When Stefan heard I was getting kudos for my quip, he'd been upset. "People will use that against you," he warned.

"You mean they don't have enough ammunition already? Like my Edith Wharton conference ending with murder instead of a closing address?"

The truth was that even if I'd never been involved in any

crime more outrageous than shoplifting, my position in EAR had always been tenuous. I was hired because I was Stefan's partner, and I taught and loved the least-respected course: composition. Though you could argue that everything else in the department rested on its foundation, it was simply too basic and boring for most EAR professors to take seriously. Even worse, most of those who had been teaching rhetoric (the "R" in EAR) before I got there were a lower caste foisted on the department through budget cutting, which deepened the general disgust for what I taught.

Even worse for me, I was good at it and consistently garnered strong student evaluations, which other faculty interpreted as pandering. But less palatable than that to many of the faculty was my status as a bibliographer, a pursuit most academics viewed as only a higher form of accounting. Certainly you needed to consult a bibliography now and then, but my profession was déclassé.

After we emptied the dishwasher and put everything away, Stefan went up to bed, and I called my cousin Sharon in New York. We'd been as close as brother and sister ever since I came out to her in my teens, but lately we'd been talking almost every day. That was because last spring she'd been diagnosed with an acoustic neuroma, a benign tumor on her auditory nerve. *Benign* was a misleading term in this case; it would continue to grow unless operated on, damaging her nerves and eventually killing her. "Quietly malignant" seemed more accurate—a stealth tumor. It wasn't technically a brain tumor, but because taking it out would involve brain surgery, that's what Stefan and I called it.

One of the best neurosurgeons in the country, who could perform the surgery Sharon needed, was at SUM's medical school, and she had consulted him back in the spring after some surgeon-shopping in New York and Boston. But since then she had been pursuing various alternatives to surgery: acupuncture, guided imagery, a macrobiotic diet, Reiki treatment, shamanism—anything to keep the scalpels away from her head. It wasn't just the ex-model in her afraid of having her beauty stolen; I would have been desperate to avoid surgery myself.

"Hi, sweetie," she said. "You guys okay?"

"We're passable." That was my compromise, since I was fine but Stefan was depressed about his career. He had what thousands of people craved: he'd published books, won some prizes, been well reviewed—and yet it had turned bitter and disappointing in ways he couldn't have imagined in the years before his career took off.

"Tell me what you had for dinner, Nick."

I did, and she sighed appropriately. "If you guys ever left teaching, you could open up a restaurant or a B&B."

"Or we could sit around and gain weight. I know for sure that inside of me is a really fat person just dying to get out."

She laughed, but stopped when I asked if she'd made a decision yet about her surgery. "I'm going to drag this out as long as I can," she said gently. "It's too big to rush into."

"Isn't it too big to wait anymore?"

"Now you sound like my parents."

"Sorry, it's just that—"

"—you're worried. I know. So am I. But I'm still not ready. Please don't nag."

"'I don't nag,'" I quoted from a famous Alka Seltzer ad in the 1960s, "'Your mother nags.'" Sharon got it, and laughed gratefully. Then she skillfully switched to dishing: "So what's new in EAR?"

"I told you Coral Greathouse got the provost's job, right?"

"Coral was the stiff?"

"That's her. And she appointed Serena Fisch—Lady Jitterbug—as acting chair, which is good for me and Stefan since she's always had a kind of soft spot for us, and I could never figure Coral out."

"But didn't Serena used to be head of some other department?"

"Sharon, you've really been working with your study guide!"

"I need one. Your department is like a soap opera."

"Maybe. There sure aren't enough pretty faces, though. But you're right, Serena *was* the chair of the Rhetoric Department when it was independent, and since it got merged with English and American Studies, she's been suffering like a deposed monarch, so her being acting chair of EAR is pretty strange."

"You mean ironic?"

I nodded.

"Well, she's lucky she got to be chair at all, and that they didn't shoot her like the Romanovs and pour acid over the corpse."

When Sharon said things like that, she reminded me more than ever of Myrna Loy in *The Thin Man*. They had the same soft, steely self-assurance, and Sharon even resembled her a bit.

"And what about Camille Cypriani?" Sharon went on. "Anything new there?"

"Not much."

Sharon had read one of Camille's novels years ago, and had told me it wasn't so much a beach read as "bathtub reading"—if you dropped the book in the water, it wasn't a great loss. I'd kept Sharon apprised of each little twist and turn of the Camille story so far, and as a research librarian (her second career), she had been struck by the quiet brutality of the Jurevicius Library being uprooted to make way for Camille.

"That woman should hire a bodyguard," Sharon said. "Really! Your campus is like a Jacobean play without the poetry. Sooner or later, somebody always gets it in the neck."

2

AFTER breakfast the next morning I headed to campus to my inglorious new office.

As if to symbolize my ambiguous status in EAR—well known and popular with students, but held in suspicion and even dreaded by some of the faculty—I'd fallen to the literal bottom of the heap. More accurately, I'd been thrown there. Having refused to stay in my office on the third floor, where so much had happened to traumatize me, I'd requested a new office before the end of the previous spring semester. But given my track record for trouble, none of the other professors wanted to share an office with EAR's version of the Ancient Mariner.

I declined Stefan's kind offer to share his grand and spacious office on the second floor, where EAR's main office was located. As EAR's writer-in-residence, Stefan had a prime corner office with views of some of the campus's loveliest walks and old buildings; it could easily have suited both of us, but I didn't think living together *and* working together would have been good for us.

So. Space had to be found for me somewhere. And it was: in

the basement. I had plummeted to the bottom. I wasn't just the only tenure-stream faculty member in EAR to have a basement office, I was the only full-time EAR professor *ever* to have been relegated to quarters below the ground floor. I'd sit there trying to work or listen to my current or prospective students and feel the entire four-story weight of that crumbling sandstone building—made heavier by the decades of squabbling, jealousy, and frustrated ambitions—hulking above me as if waiting to collapse and seal me in forever. Edgar Allen Poe meets *Dallas*.

And Parker Hall's grim basement, the home of damp and roach-ridden supply rooms and overcrowded graduate teaching assistant offices, had been made even less hospitable a place thanks to my need to move. The solution to "housing" me was to clear out a mildewed, low-ceilinged office that was probably once a broom closet and had currently been sheltering three or four TAs.

Could it get worse? Yes. I discovered that those TAs were now displaced into already cramped offices down there, where crowd-caused psychosis was likely to break out any day now. As if to highlight the graduate students' abysmal status, my office received a faculty upgrade.

The cracked, bulging walls were repainted a dismally uncheerful white, and the tiny, grotesquely pitted floor was covered over with a blackish brown carpet remnant probably found at an estate sale after a death by spontaneous combustion or a flood. To counter the soul-deep mildew, EAR even supplied a wheezing dehumidifier that was no better than some superannuated family retainer vainly wielding a feather duster in a gaping mansion. Even if the dehumidifier had worked, nothing could camouflage the reality: I had a cramped, nasty basement office with half a window, high up in the wall, that allowed little more than a view of parading shoes, boots, sandals—and the ankles attached to them. It was claustrophobic, and I spent as little time there as possible, which of course turned my office hours into even more of a freak show. I may have loathed this cargo hold of an office, but my students drank in the creepiness and said "Cool" when they took it in, as if I had just shown them a new tongue-piercing.

This descent into the abyss was doubly ironic given that my summer had been full of achievement. Working like a dervish, I had finished two projects that might possibly help get me tenure: an introduction to a new edition of Edith Wharton's neglected late novel *The Glimpses of the Moon*, and a Norton Critical Edition of her erotic novel *Summer*, which was far more interesting than its companion piece *Ethan Frome*. Whether I got tenure or not, the work was done, and valuable in its own small way.

So, heading in that Monday morning, all I could be thankful for was that EAR had no sub-basement or buried bomb shelter, or I'd have yet another level to descend. I had no problem finding a space behind Parker Hall and headed downstairs to my crypt to work on the syllabus for my upcoming mystery course. But it was hard not to shudder in the hallway, even with the lights on. The ceiling was oppressively low, the linoleum scarred and greasy, the slime-green paint peeling and chipped. I let myself into my office, feeling embarrassed, as always, by EAR's pathetic attempts to make the space more livable, turned on the buzzing overhead light and the three lamps I'd brought in, and settled down at the kind of desk you'd be ashamed to break up for firewood.

I'd been reading many dozens of mysteries and thrillers for months now and had narrowed down my course to a brief overview of the classics, including Conan Doyle and Christie, followed by a focus on PI novels, which seemed the genre's backbone, at least in the United States. I'd read somewhere that as a country born of revolution, America has always valorized "the lone outsider" lined up against established authority. In the eighteenth century that figure was the Minuteman; in the nineteenth the cowboy; and in our own it's been the PI, first vaulting to national attention in the classic crime novels of Dashiell Hammett and Raymond Chandler. It struck me as an intriguing way to focus the course, and I thought I might sneak Janet Evanovich into the more august list, which would include writers like Ross Macdonald, Lawrence Block, Michigan's own Loren D. Estleman, Dennis Lehane, and Sue Grafton.

But more importantly, teaching material that I enjoyed always made the most sense. I had been savoring these novels more than other types of mysteries, perhaps because like many readers I enjoyed imagining myself taking on the bad guys and solving the crime in a way more satisfying than if the protagonist was a librarian whose cats helped her unlock the mystery. Or the reverse: a book that threw one explosion after another at me or plunged me into the psychotic stew of a serial killer's consciousness. After half a dozen of those books, all the maniacs started sounding dismally, gruesomely alike. But my students would have the option of reading in any subgenre they wanted for their term papers, so even with a focus on PI novels, I'd still have plenty of variety in the course.

Doing a syllabus is always a small juggling act as you weigh the semester's calendar against what's a reasonable workload for the students (and yourself). You can fuss with the course forever, but eventually you have to let go. I was getting close to that stage in the process, but I wasn't there yet. Deep in calendrical calculations, I suddenly heard someone bellow out in the dismal hallway: "This is inhuman!"

I rushed to my door and saw Byron Summerscale out there. The leonine former chair of the now-defunct Department of Western Civilization (WC) was glaring, red- faced, holding a box of books and oddments, turning around slowly in the middle of the hall as if to imprint each dispiriting detail on his memory forever. He didn't seem aware of me thirty feet away.

"It's a gulag!" he cried, his voice echoing with such grief he could have been Lear contemplating Cordelia's body. Known for his tirades as much as his shoulder-length white curls, Birkenstocks, and wool socks worn practically year-round, burly Byron Summerscale was an imposing (but slightly ridiculous) Hemingwayesque figure—though I suppose you could argue that Hemingway himself was intrinsically ludicrous after a certain point in his career. I'd always thought of Summerscale as the kind of man likely to keep challenging other drunks to arm-wrestle until he collapsed under the weight of his own testosterone-driven outrage—or died of a stroke. He actually did look apoplectic right then.

"This is a hellhole!" Summerscale said, but with fading intensity. I approached and asked him what was wrong and what he was doing in Parker Hall.

He faltered. Perhaps he hadn't recognized me, so I told him my name. I'm not sure he took it in. "What am I doing here, young man? Well you may ask! I've been assigned an office down here because I'm going to be teaching in EAR now. Do you know why? Because I was given a choice: EAR, which doesn't want me, or being assigned to the dean's office."

"What does that mean?"

"It means I'd be wiping Dean Bullerschmidt's ass when he went to the crapper—that's what it means. Or just about. They're so full of spite they'd let me draw my salary for doing nothing. *Nothing.* Can you believe it?"

I didn't say what I was thinking, that many SUM professors would consider the position heavenly, but I knew that Summerscale loved teaching, and so for him it would be torture.

"And do you know where they've put me? Do you *know?*"

I dutifully shook my head, but from his frown I could tell that wasn't enough, so I said, "Where?"

"Look!" he bellowed, thrusting his chin at one side of the hallway, where a door gaped underneath black stenciled letters that read SUPPLIES. Morbidly curious, I moved toward the door and peeked inside. I may have had an actual office cleaned out for me, but Summerscale was stuck with a dark and windowless little room that looked as if it had been only cursorily cleaned before being crammed with battered furniture, chosen from SUM castoffs too ugly and damaged to sell.

"It's a supply closet," I said, feeling almost insulted by association. I wondered if the lettering over the door had been deliberately left there or was still up because of incompetence. Either possibility was a good one, though given SUM's consistent disregard for faculty, the former was likelier.

"They expect me to see students here? It's a deliberate insult. It's a *provocation.* They want me to quit! They've hacked my department to death, and now those hellhounds are after *me*." Summerscale launched into a rodomontade about his importance to the university, and I tuned out, thinking about the reality. Summerscale's physical demotion was doubtless one more sign of how little the university really cared about its students. The WC courses in Western art, philosophy, music, and literature had always been popular, as were their warm, humanistically oriented (and occasionally overdramatic) professors. But despite lip service, SUM didn't care about teaching, just money, and the anti-intellectual juggernaut rolled on. After all, this was the university that had been test-marketing a new Guiding Principle (empty slogan): Students Are Important. If SUM had to be reminded, then it was already too late.

"How can they shit on Western Civilization like this?"

I assumed he meant the department and not the tradition. WC had formerly offered one of SUM's core required courses, but over the years the university had ruthlessly whittled WC down, first by abolishing the requirement and thus cutting its student enrollments, then by chopping its budget disproportionately and consistently not hiring even temporary staff to fill vacancies left by retirement or death. Now, with only about half a dozen of the WC faculty left, the neglected and abused department had been shut down entirely without notice or any attempt to follow official university procedures. This surprise move came directly from the provost's office, and it was Coral Greathouse's first major decision.

Former chair of EAR, Greathouse was subdued but obviously already adept at upper-level maneuvering. Because the WC department was now so small (befitting its initials), and the dissolution had happened during the summer when the school newspaper didn't appear regularly, Greathouse probably expected she could get away with the purge. None of the other weary professors bothered protesting, and all took early retirement rather than be reassigned somewhere unbecoming in the College of Arts and Letters. The last I'd read, though, Summerscale's reassignment was up in the air, and there were rumors he was going to quit.

Apparently not. Which meant that I now had company in the basement. "You know, Byron, if SUM could offer drive-through courses with a side order of fries, taught by faculty earning the minimum wage, that would be the next step."

He didn't look as if smiling were even an option, but my comment diverted him into another stream of complaint. "I'm down in this atrocious pit while EAR lavishes hundreds of thousands of dollars on Camille Cypriani. An endowed chair like hers is *obscene*."

"That all depends on the upholstery," I murmured, but Summerscale, who had set down his box, was waving his arms as if addressing a throng of revolutionaries. "SUM is corrupt. What's next, a statue in her honor? Renaming Parker Hall after her? The provost is an evil woman for consenting to this business, and so is Serena Fisch for allowing Camille to infest her department. Camille Cypriani is a cancerous growth on the university's body—she must be blasted! Excised! They think I'm weak, but the Philistines thought Samson was weak—and look how he buried them in their own venom!"

Summerscale kept on raving in this vein, mixing metaphors as he went, while I contemplated the politics involved. I suspected that Serena's acquiescence had been purchased by the offer of acting chair, with the assurance that she would keep the position no matter who ran against her, provided she didn't question the position for Cypriani. This fix was possible because the dean had to approve departmental elections for chair and had in the past chosen the losing candidate for various reasons.

"Nicholas," Summerscale said, turning to me with as much fervor as if I were his savior, "we have to fight this outrage. We have to oust Cypriani from her position. It's the ruin of SUM. "

Who did he think he was? Cato calling for the fall of Carthage?

"They may have tossed me into this cesspool, but I will not be silenced! If the only thing I can do is destroy their complacency—that's enough! Will you help me, Nicholas?"

I didn't bother explaining that my full name was actually Nick. But I did say, "Byron, I'm too junior a faculty member. I'm

untenured. And I've had, well, a few murky years in EAR.
There's nothing I can do." Not that I wanted to follow Byron
Summerscale onto a barricade anyway, though the idea of him
as a gadfly pleased me. Too many faculty on campus kept their
heads down, avoided confrontation, and let the administration
rule as brutally as Byzantine emperors who blinded and exiled
their opponents.

Summerscale gave me his impression of a basilisk. It was
pretty good.

"Really, Byron, I'm sorry I can't help you."

Summerscale actually growled at me, and I wondered if he
would make it through the semester without an ambulance carting him off for observation, or if I would escape being bitten or
mauled.

Trying manfully to lighten the atmosphere, I said, "With
both of us down here now, maybe somebody will study us, you
know, and write a thesis: 'Debasement in the Basement.' " He
didn't respond, which made me reckless. "The personal is political, right? So why don't we form an Academics Anonymous
group? Our first step would be trying to rise out of the basement—emotionally."

His face twisted with disgust, Summerscale said, "You're a
collaborator. You're a stooge!"

Offended, I was tempted to ask which one of the Three
Stooges Summerscale meant, but wisely I retreated to my office
and closed the door. Out in the hall I heard a loud "She's de-
stroying this university!" followed by a slamming door. Who did
Summerscale mean? Camille Cypriani? Coral Greathouse?
Xena, Warrior Princess?

Looking around, I luxuriated in the awareness that my new
digs weren't as bad as I'd thought. At least my office was clean,
carpeted, and had half a window, as opposed to none at all.
What was once dreary and depressing suddenly felt unconscio-
nably plush. How could I be dissatisfied when practically right
outside my door was a worse example of the university's mis-
treatment of faculty?

But wasn't it wrong to be at all complacent? Once again, I

found myself reflecting on the ways in which SUM was a corrupt and corrupting place to work, that what people learned to take for granted there ended up deadening their feelings. And *this* is where I wanted tenure.

There was a knock on my door, and I hesitated, hoping that Summerscale hadn't come down the hall to remonstrate with me some more, but it was Betty and Bill Malatesta, who shared one of the fiercely overcrowded offices down the hall and used to be in the office that had been cleared out for me. They were both tall, blond, athletic, and as stylish as TAs can get on a tight budget—EAR's low-rent Bogey and Bacall. But they'd been looking a bit faded and querulous lately, stuck in EAR an extra year when they should have been out in academia with good tenure-track jobs.

Feeling like a trespasser, I invited them in and asked what was up. They stood just inside the door, and I cringed as each of them subtly took in the changes to what was once their office.

"We heard the altercation," Betty said. "Are you okay?" There was a languid prurience in her concern, as if she had idly hoped to find me in need of rescue or relief, and had already cast herself as the star of a dramatic anecdote. Despite being the smartest and most productive of the department's TAs, the Malatestas were at the very bottom of the heap in EAR, working with pathetic salaries, lousy benefits, and constant stress. Treated like serfs by many of the professors, they were part of EAR's proletariat, and particularly restless now.

"Why wouldn't I be okay?"

"Dr. Summerscale can get violent," Betty said with buoyant neutrality, as if she were reporting on a meteorological phenomenon. "That's why his wife divorced him." She seemed to wait for my prompting to divulge lubricious details, but I said nothing, and she twisted her pretty shoulders a bit as if annoyed. "I mean, it's not that I don't admire him, but he's also very careless."

"Careless?"

Betty leaned forward confidingly. "He invites students to bars in town for conferences."

"To seduce them?" It seemed ludicrous—Summerscale was anything but subtle or charming.

She grinned and shook her head. "No. To drink."

Bill nodded and said, "Summerscale can be very inappropriate."

I wondered what could be more inappropriate than drinking with your students, but wasn't sexual. Drugs? Mail fraud? Amway?

Stefan would never be having this conversation, I was sure. He would tell me that I shouldn't have been gossiping about another faculty member with TAs, but I was curious now just the same. "What do you mean by very inappropriate?"

Bill deflected my question with a joke he claimed was making the rounds: "They say Camille's chair is funded by a large endowment. Does that mean it comes with well-hung drapes?" Betty mock-slapped Bill—"What a shitty pun!"—and they left without saying anything more about Summerscale, though their eyes raked the room's improvements one last time, making me feel even more uncomfortable than before about having displaced them.

Doing graduate studies in EAR, as in most departments, is an exercise in being a worm. Professors who have been ill-treated in their own academic apprenticeships continue the abuse with their own students as if mired in some Balkan vendetta whose hold can never be broken. Trying to counter that coldness, I had tried to be friendly to Bill and Betty, with mixed results in the past. And now that I had usurped their office, nothing I did would make a difference.

Both of the Malatestas had been stars in the Ph.D. program, publishing articles, doing conference papers, seemingly destined for good positions. But despite all their job interviews at MLA the previous year and the campus follow-ups, I knew that they were still unemployed, and resentment flickered behind their charming smiles. Neither had defended their dissertation yet, so as to be able to teach one more year; they needed the money, and EAR was always hungry for cheap labor, whether in the form of TAs or adjunct professors. It was a vile arrangement, but the way universities were headed everywhere around the country.

The theory is that graduate school teaches you to be a member of the profession. They'd certainly been well trained—in envy.

I tried working on my syllabus some more, but gave it up, feeling too jangled by the morning's unexpected interruptions. I decided to head to the gym without even checking my mail. Just packing up and turning out the lights made me feel I was taking action, but even a quick getaway didn't help me escape more bad vibes.

Just outside Parker, I almost bumped into one of EAR's gypsy scholars, Cassius "Cash" Jurevicius, who was heading inside toward his own Dickensian office in the basement, which he shared with TAs. I apologized perhaps too effusively, since I was always a bit unnerved by his potty, feral good looks that made him resemble a dark-haired Ryan Philippe.

He shrugged dismissively, frowned, mumbled something, and ducked around me into Parker. Like his namesake in *Julius Caesar*, Cash always looked lean and hungry, and most days he barely said hello to me now. Heading for my Taurus, I sighed, even though I understood that his resentment wasn't really personal, since Cash loathed all tenure-track faculty. He had a Ph.D. from the University of Chicago, and his grandmother had been the much-loved chair of English and American Studies in the 1950s. Cash's specialty was Lacan, Derrida, Kristeva, and all those other French bullies, so I knew it was particularly galling to him that he was only an adjunct teaching low-level courses in a department and college where his family has been honored and esteemed.

As I got into my car, I thought it had been a typical morning at EAR: another parade of misfits and malcontents.

3

I COULD leave that all behind, I thought, with a short drive to Michiganapolis's world-class health club. Palatial, but unimaginatively named, the Club sprawled quite near campus on a wooded, ten-acre site like some lush little private college. Expensive, expansive, it housed vast arrays of the latest weight-training and aerobic exercise machines, tennis courts, indoor and outdoor pools, twin basketball courts, dozens of racquetball and squash courts, plush shower rooms with sauna, Jacuzzi, and steam rooms—everything but a bowling alley and a flight simulator. Though its members were a range from fit to fat, it was still a self-absorbed and absorbing little universe.

I'd found a new interest there since Sharon got sick, or rediscovered an old one. I'd begun swimming again after many years because it seemed the best release of tension possible as I moved slowly but steadily through the cool water, which muffled noise and made me feel weightless, free, if only for half an hour. I also had come to prefer time in the pool to working out with weights because I wasn't even implicitly competing with buffed Stefan when I swam.

As I changed downstairs in the overbright locker room into the baggy old swim trunks that were surprisingly stylish again (and nowhere near as embarrassing for me as a Speedo), put my stuff away, and headed off to shower before entering the pool, I remembered Byron Summerscale's bombast. Showering off and putting on my goggles, I felt annoyed at his tirade and abuse, but by the time I had padded along to the Olympic-size lap pool to do some stretches, I was ashamed of myself.

It was the problem I'd been worrying about last year: wasn't exposure to the department and the university's cynicism desensitizing me? I should have been deeply outraged by SUM's treatment of Summerscale. After all, the former WC chair had a distinguished teaching career at the university, he'd written several well-received books, and surely attention must be paid to such a man. Even though he was silly around the edges and self-dramatizing, that was no excuse for me to ignore him or SUM to humiliate him.

I couldn't help thinking of a Don DeLillo novel, *Players*, in which a New York character deliberately yawns when she's angry and stressed and dismisses it all as "boring." Is that where I was headed? Would I just wave off the university's brutality and keep my head down even if I had tenure? Was that a way to live?

The lap pool wasn't very crowded late morning, and I could have a lane to myself. After getting hand paddles, a kickboard and a pool buoy, I did some "skips": two laps each of swimming, kicking, "pulling" with the buoy between my legs, and more swimming. Gradually, thankfully, I set aside the new example of university injustice I'd just had my face rubbed in. I reveled in my momentary freedom and ease, and the quickly renewed pleasure of having found something that really kept me in shape.

Some days in the pool I had to remind myself to reach, *reach*, or my breathing was ragged, or I could feel that my kick was inefficient, that I was splashing more than necessary, or that I was starting my kick turn too soon—but today none of that happened. It turned into an ideal swim, where I felt not just completely at home in the water but part of it, inseparable.

After twenty laps, I decided to take a short rest at the shallow end, enjoying the pump in my chest and shoulders, the way my breathing felt stronger, deeper. It was always very erotic to feel the cool water against my reddened chest.

As I stood there, leaning back against the lip of the pool, my goggles down around my neck and the air filling with a kind of fugue of splashing, I realized that feisty and foulmouthed Juno Dromgoole was in the next lane. Now, *she* was an EAR faculty member I was always happy to run into. As an assistant professor without tenure, I had to be circumspect, so I wallowed in Juno's bravado and absolute lack of bullshit. Juno had been visiting professor of Canadian literature last year but was now permanent in EAR, since Coral Greathouse had chosen her to fill Serena Fisch's position. Juno was even freer to speak her mind honestly this year, though she was the kind of woman who would always say what she thought.

Juno was violently against anything she termed political correctness, and consistently inveighed against what she rightly considered a hypocritical and mealy-mouthed department. Juno also didn't hold with Cypriani's endowed chair, having loudly called EAR's deluxe new faculty member an "overpriced hack." Despite this popular stance, many faculty didn't want rude Juno around, but she'd been granted tenure, so EAR was stuck with her.

That pleased me. If I couldn't make the bastards squirm, I was glad somebody could—and so stylishly. And right then, in the pool, I watched her with admiration: she had an enviably smooth stroke and a terrific, easy kick-turn. It wasn't the kind of grace I would have expected of her. She seemed so much a creature of stiletto heels, tight skirts, and revealing blouses—equal parts Chaka Khan, Bette Midler, and Tina Turner. I decided to linger a little longer before doing some more skips, and then Juno stopped at my end of the pool, pulled off her goggles, and grinned: "Nick! I've never seen you here before!"

Juno was by far EAR's most colorful and provocative faculty member, and looked sexy in a very Esther Williams gold mesh one-piece with matching swim cap, though Williams would never have shown that much cleavage. As my Belgian parents might have said if they deigned to pay her any attention, Juno had "*tout le monde au balcon.*" She was mighty stacked.

We chatted about our schedules and how marvelous the facilities were at the Club, while the wakes of other people's workouts swept our way, knocking us every now and then gently off our feet. But instead of listening completely, I found myself watching her, distracted by her deep cleavage, full lips, and golden-clad hips. I had to work to focus on her conversation. What the hell was going on with me?

"I love swimming," she was saying. "I imagine I've gone down with a ship and I'm the only one who's escaping. What makes it perfect is that the rest of the ship is filled with horrors from our department. I'm sure you know who I mean. It's *very* satisfying."

I don't think that's the kind of guided imagery you find on healing and empowerment tapes, but it sounded uplifting to me. It could probably do quite well at the MLA convention.

We grinned at each other, and the light flickering on the water and its multitude of reflections seemed focused at her eyes and her bright, even teeth. And that's when I was suddenly as sharply aware of how close we were standing as if I'd been watching myself on screen. There was so little between us—just water, a blue plastic lane rope, and a little fabric.

Juno reached over and with two fingers brushed hair back from my forehead.

"That's better—now I can see your eyes. Hugh Grant hair is all well and good, but eyes like yours should never be obscured."

"Oh. Thanks." At that moment, I would not have been surprised if she had touched me again, but what did surprise me was wanting to feel her hand on my face.

"You're blushing," Juno said, her voice low and silky.

That made my face turn even darker red—I could feel the heat of it.

"But don't stop on my account," she said.

Last year I had found her outrageousness refreshing in a department full of cranky has-beens, but now my awareness of her sexuality wasn't theoretical, it was surprisingly visceral. She had somehow moved from being a riot to arousing. It was in its own way as thrilling a discovery as the first time another man had touched me and I entered a different realm of being. But it was far more threatening.

"Does your chest always flush when you're swimming?" she asked. "It was red before your face was."

I nodded.

"It's lovely—and I suppose the same thing happens in bed."

My face wasn't alone in responding to Juno, and I was appalled at losing control of my body. Trying to be discreet, I dropped a hand down in front of my trunks before she could notice anything else. Thank God I wasn't wearing a Speedo.

"You're very trim," she said. "You wouldn't know it seeing you scuttle around Parker Hall. But then that's with clothes on."

I managed a comeback. "Parker makes everyone look bad," I said, wondering if I did indeed scuttle. Probably so, compared to Juno, who loved stalking through the halls in a cloud of Albert Sung, her own private—and victorious—procession.

Her eyes were hooded.

"Everyone except you," I added, and she smiled languidly. I flushed again. Was I flirting with her? It was a first.

"You know," Juno said, "I was watching you swim. I could help you with your stroke."

I coughed and debated about moving my other hand down under the water, and Juno added, "You only have to ask. I was a lifeguard as a teenager—"

Suddenly the door from the men's locker room thundered open, and we turned. Dean Bullerschmidt surged through, looking murderous. Workaholic, power-hungry Bullerschmidt was renowned at SUM for driving people crazy with relentless e-mails and early-morning meetings. In utterly shapeless swim trunks as large as a flag, he thudded along the tiled floor to our end of the pool, almost knocking over a young lifeguard without apologizing, his grotesque, fat-flapping, ruined body looming like a leaking parade float. He said nothing to me, and without even asking Juno if he could share her lane (which was standard pool etiquette), Bullerschmidt angrily crashed down into the pool, the wave of water almost sending me and Juno under.

"Vile bastard," Juno said, not remotely *sotto voce*, as SUM's answer to the Borgias proceeded to water-walk down to the other end of the pool as briskly as a man of his enormous bulk could do. He was as large as John Candy, but there was nothing really ingratiating or the least bit goofy about him—every pound seemed like a brick in a tower from which he meant to pour boiling oil on his enemies, and maybe even his friends, if he had any.

"He's hideous," Juno said to me, staring after our elephantine dean with morbid fascination, while the other swimmers in the pool went back to their routines.

It was clearly exercise, but I was horrified by the way the dean stalked along as if trampling someone very specific underfoot. Bullerschmidt was probably one of SUM's cruelest administrators, but his viciousness was usually much more restrained.

"What's made him so furious?" I asked.

"A man like that doesn't need a reason—looking in the mirror every morning would be enough."

No, I thought, there had to be more going on. Was something happening at SUM, or worse, in the College of Arts and Letters, that was going to affect me and Stefan?

We watched him, appalled.

"You know," Juno said, "I heard women in our locker room talking about him one day. He'd had some kind of altercation with another club member in the pool recently and threatened to punch him out. He's also argued with people in the men's sauna and whirlpool and gotten violent." Juno added that she'd also heard there had been complaints about the dean's belligerence from other members, but the Club was unwilling to take any steps against so powerful an SUM figure. "It's not enough that he's a fucking offensive turd. He'd have to hurt someone badly first," she said.

"Right. It's just like a stop sign not getting put up at a dangerous corner until there's an accident." Last year I had suspected the dean of murder on campus, based on his volcanic hostility, and watching him now, I felt my judgment of his potential hadn't been wrong. It was clear he wasn't just prepared to cut people off at the legs administratively.

"SUM's finest," I said bitterly.

"He's a monster, and there's only one reason to go to his fucking reception for Camille tonight: maybe we'll get lucky, and he'll choke to death or keel over with a stroke. And crush that Cypriani creature when he falls."

Juno and I hurriedly left the pool before Bullerschmidt made his return trip down to our end, arranging to have lunch together in the Club's restaurant after we were dressed. I showered quickly, unsettled by having found Juno so alluring and afraid I'd spring up under my own soapy hands like a teenager. On the way back to my locker, I passed a guy from SUM's tennis team who looked a lot like William Baldwin. I'd never seen him in just a towel before, and as he padded by, I discreetly checked him out.

Good, I thought with relief. I was still normal despite that strange interlude in the pool.

Upstairs in the restaurant that was so dark it was in need of a bitter, world-weary chanteuse boa'd over the bar, I waited for Juno, grossed out and a little alarmed at having seen Dean Bullerschmidt's veneer of civility scraped away with his clothes. But more importantly, I thought, drinking a second glass of water to rehydrate myself, what had been going on for me in the pool with Juno? I'd rarely if ever even noticed a woman sexually. Had my appreciation of Juno's rampant theatricality over the past year really been something else all along—an unconscious physical attraction? Or was this some weird sort of midlife crisis coming on? It sure wasn't diva worship. I didn't want to trade fashion tips or hand her flowers like some queen at a Patti Labelle concert, I *wanted* her.

As if my thoughts had been broadcast over a loudspeaker, I glanced nervously around the crowded red and green restaurant. It was filled with suited realtors, lawyers, doctors, and local politicos for whom membership at the Club and a locker with their name on it was a status symbol, though they came in mostly for lunch or dinner, with only an occasional game of tennis or racquetball, which was long enough to leave their towels on the floor and neglect to flush the urinals.

In one corner a giant TV with the sound way down broadcast some widemouthed, overly eager commentator on ESPN. Everyone else was chatting and eating. Nobody was looking at me. Good.

I had not struggled as much as many people do with my sexuality because I realized I was gay very early. I was lucky enough to have a psychoanalyst in New York who'd called my parents into her office—hung with Japanese prints she'd bought at Sotheby's—and said they could either embrace my being gay or make me and themselves crazy by fighting it. With their European reverence for Freud and the profession he spawned, my mother and father accepted this warning, and with it, my sexual identity, more easily than even I did at first.

While I waited for Juno to stalk through the door, I was surprised to see Bill and Betty Malatesta again. Bill sauntered over to my table and asked, "How many professors with endowed chairs does it take to change a lightbulb?"

Dutifully, I asked how many.

"None," he snarled in a passable imitation of Camille Cypriani. "Change it yourself, asshole!"

I usually enjoyed his jokes, but this one came out sounding too brittle. Still, I tried making conversation. "How long have you guys been members here?"

Betty said, "Oh, we're not members, we just come to the restaurant to see how the other half lives."

Bill was as embarrassed by her bitterness as I was, and he dragged Betty off to a table around the corner of the bar.

Juno showed up just then, with her black leather gym bag, perfectly coiffed, in stacked heels and a tight black jumpsuit with a wide leopard-print belt, drawing everyone's eyes. As she settled into a chair at my left, pulling around the place setting from opposite me, I almost felt we were on some kind of date, even though this meeting was completely casual. Or was it?

A multiply pierced waitress who looked like Olive Oyl drifted over and announced that she was Sherry.

"Do you have any proof?" Juno asked severely, stumping the young girl completely.

"Uh . . . Can I get you anything?" Sherry tried.

Juno swept the room with her vodka gimlet glance and suggested we order Heinekens and club sandwiches, which was fine with me. Sherry decamped.

"That bartender looks too incompetent to mix ingredients. Beer shouldn't be too taxing for him," Juno announced. "Though he does look a bit like Leonardo DiCaprio. And wasn't *that* a disappointing movie? *Titanic*. And a bloody waste of time." She continued before I could agree or object. "All the magazines said Leonardo was the hot new thing, and I wanted to see the hot, the new, and his thing. But it was all so fucking decorous. As for his lover—what a whiny cow! Why couldn't *she* have died?"

I laughed, even though Stefan and I had both been so shaken by *Titanic,* we had sat there through the entire thing almost motionless. Both of us had imagined losing the other, and cried. This was one of the things I loved best about Stefan. He had cried the first time we saw *Dark Victory* together, and even more so when we watched it over the summer, thinking about Sharon's brain tumor.

Juno wriggled her shoulders in appreciation of my approval and happily blasted the movie some more, targeting its many anachronisms. When our beers came, though, she leaned forward conspiratorially and said, "We have to talk about Camille Cypriani—and the dean! Going to his reception honoring that phony tonight is an even more noisome prospect than before. Now that I've seen that Loch Ness monster practically in the nude, it'll destroy my appetite completely. I cannot stand men who've let their bodies collapse like that."

I nodded, and she eyed me.

"I like men built like you. Big legs to wrap around my neck. A tight chest to pound on—or scratch."

I tried gulping down some beer, feeling a bit dazed. "Why are you being so flirtatious?"

"Why are you enjoying it?" she asked, but I shook my head, refusing to comment, and she said, "It's quite simple. I've never seen you in the pool before. I've never seen so much of you. And I like a challenge." Her smile was just close enough to a leer to make me think she'd noticed I'd had the makings of a hard-on in the pool. But jeez, did it have to be something that obvious? Maybe Juno was picking up that for the first time since we'd known each other, I was turned on by something more than her take-no-prisoners energy.

I suddenly felt more exposed there at the table than I had in the pool, and all sorts of vague and threatening possibilities whirled around us. But Juno backtracked and started railing against Camille Cypriani's exorbitant salary, sounding as bitter as everyone else in EAR. I agreed with her but said that complaining wouldn't make a difference.

"Of course it won't!" Juno practically snarled. "We can't just talk about her—we have to *destroy* that woman." She suddenly grabbed my hand, and before I could pull it away, she hissed, "I have something important to tell you. I'm planning to run for EAR department chair against Serena Fisch."

Just then Sherry nervously deposited our sandwiches, as if she were afraid Juno would grab *her*.

"But she's your friend. She got you the visiting professorship last year."

Juno released my hand. Her eyes went wide, and her beautiful French-manicured hands worked themselves into fists I thought she was going to pound on the table. Very softly, she said, "I'm the one who got that post. As for Serena being my friend, not now, not anymore, not when she rolls over for the provost and the dean and lets them shove Camille Cypriani down our throats. I wanted you to be the first to know about my plans because I'm sure you'll support me."

She leaned back and drained half of her beer. "As EAR chair, I intend to combat Camille's hiring and undo it—somehow."

I didn't see how that was possible, but if Juno did run, the department was headed for a meltdown.

"You'll vote for me, won't you, Nick?"

What a mess. As acting chair, Serena was even more involved with my tenure review than before, so how could I vote against her? Serena had also saved my hide two years ago when she helped me organize the department's conference on Edith Wharton. Yet I wasn't convinced she'd be the best candidate for chair, given that she had turned very high-handed and authoritarian in just the short time she'd been acting chair. I would actually relish outspoken Juno in a position of power; she'd be much less willing to put up with the status quo and could possibly do the department some good.

Surprised, embarrassed, confused, I said I couldn't promise anything, and Juno eyed me coldly before smiling. "I hope you'll reconsider. After all, you don't have tenure, do you?"

I chomped on my sandwich. I thought about how perplexing this development was. Ordinarily, Juno would have gone back to Canada at the end of the previous academic year, but now EAR was stuck with her for the long haul. What was Coral Greathouse thinking when she appointed Serena acting chair and gave Juno tenure—was she lobbing a grenade into the department? And if so, why?

Juno quietly sipped her beer now as if she'd passed through some kind of crisis. I watched her lick the foam off her lips, imagining doing it myself. God, I was really screwed up! And the thought of Serena and Juno vying against each other for chair was very disturbing; the last thing EAR needed was its own Clash of the Titans. Though she had administrative experience, Serena's appointment and her inevitable candidacy for chair when her term ran out was already exacerbating the long and bitter divide between EAR's "first-class" and "second-class" faculty—all the former Rhetoric Department people who were constantly ill-treated and dissed. Serena would obviously count on all of those people as her core voters, and since Rhetoric faculty happened to constitute my tenure review committee, I had been expecting the strong-arming to start any day. I also expected to give in.

But voting against Juno if she did run would leave me with an unforgiving enemy whether she won or not. She'd find out—I didn't depend on anybody's vote staying secret.

"I have to go," Juno dropped, rising gracefully, regally, and with a hint of menace.

"I'll pay," I offered.

"This time, yes." Juno grabbed her gym bag and turned to go. I watched her black-clad hips as she glided off, and breathed in the perfume that still filled the air around our table. I paid as soon as I was done a few minutes later, and headed out to the parking lot. But before I could open up my car door, I saw what looked like a folded-up flyer tucked well under one windshield wiper. Had it been there before? It was low enough not to be visible from inside the car. I set down my bag, reached for the crimson folded sheet, and opened what I assumed would be an ad for house painting or dietary supplements or something like that.

It was a message in fat block computer-generated letters:

YOU DESERVE TO DIE.

4

I WHIRLED around the empty parking lot like a bullied teenager about to be pounced on by his tormentors. But as far as I could tell, there wasn't anyone lurking to see my reaction, and there weren't similar flyers on any of the dozens of cars gleaming in the sun around me. So this wasn't a Michiganapolis outbreak of Millennium Fever. It was surely personal. Someone was trying to make me mad, and it was working.

Furious, I opened up the driver's-side door, flung my bag inside, and peeled out of the lot. If it hadn't been there when I left campus, then someone going in or out of the Club had put it there. I drove a purple Taurus—easy enough to identify, since it looked like a little spaceship with rounded edges, windows, and even instrument panel. But who was behind this? A former student I'd given a bad grade to? Or worse, one of the Malatestas, angry about losing their decent-sized office and focusing their professional frustrations on me? That didn't make sense, since I'd always been friendly to them. But EAR was not an environment where even the smallest good deeds were rewarded; the tide of bitterness swept too high.

Could the note have been left by Juno, playing some kind of head game on me by flirting, then attacking? No—that didn't make sense either, since she was not given to surreptitious moves, and had even boldly announced that last year, with operatic assertiveness, when I suspected her of harassing another faculty member. I still remembered her shouting in our kitchen: "Does anyone in his right mind think that I have to send you a postcard if I think you're a worthless piece of shit? *Me*?" And she had punctuated the cry by smacking her bust and letting out a wild "Hah!" The only things missing were some pounding Stravinsky and dry ice fog.

No, not Juno. It wasn't her style. Besides, the note had been prepared in advance.

But I was so jangled by the bizarre note that I was on automatic pilot and suddenly found myself heading onto campus instead of driving home. I cursed, then decided I might as well get my mail, since I was halfway back to Parker Hall.

Checking my mail at the EAR office over the summer had become an irritating reminder of my ambivalent new status. Before the office changeover, I would climb to the second floor, then head up to the third. But now, getting to my office was always going to mean a descent to the very Stygian depths.

Not that the EAR office was much better. Because our department was not important to the university (i.e., it didn't bring in grant money), it was underfunded and poorly housed. It's grant money that provides major funding for SUM, since the university can take close to 50 per cent right off the top for "operating expenses." That meant providing essential equipment like air and water. It was a shakedown, but at least nobody's kneecaps got busted, just their pride.

EAR's main office demonstrated anything-but-benign neglect, from the gouged and buckling dingy linoleum, past the mucus-green peeling walls, and up to the ceiling with enough cracks in it to read like a road map if they'd been colored in. Someone had recently replaced shabby travel posters of English castles and gardens with Michigan posters—the Mackinac Bridge, Grand Traverse Bay, Tahquamenon Falls in the Upper

Peninsula, Soaring Eagle Casino in Mt. Pleasant—but their gleaming surfaces and uncurled edges threw the office's decrepitude into much higher relief, like a cashmere sweater on a bag lady. And the posters sent the absolute wrong message, I thought—the beauty and promise were all outside, and there was nothing here.

Entering this *sanctum dolorum*, I nodded to the secretaries off behind the forbiddingly tall linoleum-topped counter teeming with departmental flyers and schedules. I turned to my box, digging out mail, flyers, notes. And at the rear, all the way at the rear, was a paperback. I fished it out. It was a copy of the Penguin Dante's *Inferno*, and it stank.

There was no note, no inscription, and the paperback actually smelled disgustingly smoky, as if it had been in an oven, or stuck in a pail of fireplace ashes. I held it up and asked, "Who put this here?"

Three pairs of secretarial eyes took me in coldly, critically. I had raised my voice. This was not done. But I waved the smelly book at the secretaries, and they reared back at their desks as if I were going to shy it over the counter. Then their leader, Dulcie Halligan, a white-haired Barbara Bush wannabe, rose with her perpetual martyred look, advanced a few steps toward the counter, and glared defiantly at me as if she were Joan of Arc and I the invading Britons. But she said nothing.

That was a surprise, because she often responded to the simplest queries as if they were offensive comments about her parentage. And oddly, each time she felt the need to inform you that she had graduated from SUM "cum laude." I waited for this riposte, and she stared some more.

I ended the standoff by tossing the book into the nearest trash basket, where it thudded to the bottom, and stomping out of the office. I let the door bang behind me despite the large sign that asked people to "be gentle with our door."

"Shit," I mumbled, clambering down the stairs and out of the building. "They treat doors better than people here."

But outside, as I laid my mail down on the passenger's seat and started up my car, I wondered about the meaning of the crude jokes someone was playing on me. The flyer and the book had to be part of the same message, didn't they? As I turned out onto the evergreen-lined Michigan Avenue for the short drive home, I considered what exactly was the intent behind these communications, one stark, the other a bit more subtle. The book seemed to be a nasty jibe about my having a basement office, wasn't it? People in EAR did jest about the basement as the Lost World and otherwise mock its steamy depths and the people whose offices were there.

But maybe someone was saying, Go to hell. Okay, why, and who? Was there some religious fanatic in the faculty who thought I was damned? Then why wait so long to tell me? I'd been here four years and was going into my fifth. It couldn't have been anyone new, either, could it? There was only Camille Cypriani, and I don't think I even registered with her as a human being worth noticing.

The flyer was loud, angry—whereas putting that smoke-ridden book in my box was far more sophisticated. To buy the book, ensure that it smelled suitably of brimstone—all that took some malicious, thoughtful planning. Could two different people be after me somehow, or was someone trying to make me even more paranoid by creating the impression of more than one opponent?

I calmed down a bit when I drove up to our house, a pretty center-hall Colonial on the kind of green and quiet street you often see in thrillers like *Face/Off* in which ordinary people's lives explode with improbabilities. Unexpectedly, I found myself chuckling: maybe what had happened wasn't really mean-spirited—maybe the Dante paperback was an early party favor for the hellish reception that evening in honor of Camille Cypriani. Maybe several faculty members in EAR had received similar tokens, and it would all be explained tonight. I could use the laughs; these shindigs were always as grim and unpleasant as departmental meetings, just camouflaged with refreshments, but we couldn't stay away.

Sitting there in my Taurus, it suddenly hit me that I couldn't recall what I'd done with the rotten flyer. I rifled through my pockets, tore through the pile of mail, opened the car doors, and looked under the seats. I tried calming down and closing my eyes to take myself through each moment before and after its discovery, but that was useless and made me even edgier. Had I left the flyer in the parking lot at the Club—or dropped it somewhere in Parker Hall? Had I been so angry I'd unconsciously balled it up and thrown it away? Why couldn't I remember?

Frustrated and annoyed at my forgetfulness, I grabbed my briefcase, my mail, and my gym bag and headed inside, wondering how to tell Stefan about this harassment, if that was the right word for what had happened. Should I even bring it up at all? Last year, when my new officemate and our neighbor across the street Lucille had been racially harassed, it had deeply troubled Stefan, triggering feelings about his parents' suffering in the Holocaust.

From the living room I heard *Les Portes de Souvenir* by Les Nubians playing, and I wondered if Stefan had put on the dreamy, jazzy "Afropean" music to sedate himself because he was upset. I played that CD when I was relaxed and wanted to chill some more, but Stefan played it when he was stressed out.

I found him in the kitchen, silent, concentrating as he spooned tablespoon-sized mounds of very shiny dough onto nonstick baking sheets. He was barefoot, wearing olive cutoffs and a kelly green tank top.

"Gougères?" I asked, eyeing the bowls near the sink, sniffing the air.

He nodded, methodically brushing the tops with the milk left over from the batter, then sprinkling them with grated Gruyère. The first batch went into the oven, and he turned with a mildly welcoming grin. He set the oven timer for twenty-five minutes. "Have a good morning?"

I set down my gym bag and briefcase, put my mail near the phone. "Not exactly. I—"

But Stefan wasn't listening; he was already rechecking the cookbook. Gougères, cheese puffs, were not that hard to make, but they took concentration, time, and effort, and we didn't bake them that often.

"Are those for the reception tonight?"

He shook his head as if he'd just walked into a spiderweb. "Are you kidding? I wouldn't bring Camille a bag of cheese *popcorn*. These are for us." He pointed to the table. "I chilled a bottle of that Von Strasser Napa Valley Chardonnay you like."

I did—it was fruity and as crisp as a Chablis, but I begged off, explaining that I had already had a beer at lunch with Juno, at the Club.

"Juno." Stefan didn't like her, found her melodramatic and obnoxious. How could she be Canadian? he once asked. Weren't they supposed to be genteel and quiet? I had not pointed out that this was an unenlightened comment, not that I cared much. Juno's brassiness, her overturning of stereotypes, was what drew me to her.

"So what's with the gougères?" I asked, not wanting to discuss Juno right then, since our interactions in the pool and at lunch had been so murky—for me, anyway; Juno didn't seem at all perturbed until I said I couldn't promise I'd vote for her. "What happened today, Stefan? Why are you cooking so early?"

Stefan's shoulders sunk a little and he dropped into a chair. "I had a long talk with my agent."

Oh God, the perpetual messenger who deserved to be shot.

"That is, he talked, and I listened. He's given up on the book. Nobody's interested even when they like the writing, the idea, the characters. They all say the same thing: they're not convinced of its potential."

I groaned, even though I'd heard all this before. Publishing suffered from the Big Book syndrome. Every book had to have the potential to make it to the best-seller lists. But there was a major problem with this thinking. There just weren't enough readers out there—so how could every book be expected to knock one out of the park?

"Why did I ever go for a degree in creative writing? I should have stayed with French. I won my high school's French award. I met the French ambassador in New York. He shook my hand—he gave me a certificate. I never got less than an A in any French class. I was terrific."

Stefan's facts were unassailable, but he'd never expressed regret about having chosen writing over French before, so it was hard for me to take this seriously. And I knew that he'd have been even less happy teaching French at the university level, since it was a shrinking, embattled field, and he would have been crushed long before this point in his life, sinking like the French nobles at Agincourt.

"So what's his advice?" I asked. "Go with a small press?"

"No. He wants me to try something new, since I'm not getting anywhere."

I sat next to him. "Something new—like what?"

Stefan shook his head, looking baffled. "He thinks I should try writing a thriller."

I snorted—what an idiotic idea. Explosions, conspiracies, rampant betrayals, fast pacing, nerve-racking plot twists, were antithetical to Stefan's taste in literature and to his fictional vision. He might come along to that kind of movie with me, but he watched it from a critical distance and picked out plot flaws as keenly as an IRS agent combing through tax returns for evidence of fraud. Stefan had been sampling some thrillers in the last six months only because I was working on the syllabus for my mystery course in the spring, and he was curious. But forget about reading one all the way through—Stefan had always said he'd much rather spend his evenings with Balzac, Henry James, D. H. Lawrence, or Anita Brookner. Or me.

He didn't think much of PI novels either. "This is unreal," he kept saying, especially when I'd rave about one and he'd try it for a few chapters. "PIs mostly do background investigations," he said. "Or divorce work—they don't go around blowing up their enemies. They don't *have* enemies—they have business rivals."

"But that wouldn't make an interesting book, would it?"

"Exactly. And what's with all the psychotic sidekicks? There are enough of them to form a union local. Did they all go to the same boot camp, or have weekend retreats together to network?"

Even though that made me laugh, I felt a bit defensive about the subgenre. "Come on, Stefan, you know the wacko sidekicks are there to do things the heroes can't."

"So much for heroism." He shrugged. "But even if they did all that stuff, it would be unreal, and it bores me."

"But fiction *is* unreal."

"Not when it's good. You're telling me that all those Edith Wharton books you read are unreal, impossible, untrue to life?"

He had me there. I did not, however, point out Stefan's major new blind spot. He had recently purchased a DVD of *Sudden Death*, the Jean-Claude Van Damme thriller set at a hockey stadium, which we had caught one night on HBO when there was nothing else on. He had since the purchase watched it once a week. I would never have imagined that Stefan could become obsessed with Van Damme's next-to-unbelievable bravery. It had been bad enough over the summer that Stefan read pick-me-ups like *The Magic Mountain* and *Jude the Obscure*, but it was worse contemplating his enjoyment when the villains in *Sudden Death* got stabbed, torched, or blown up. Though I suppose in his own defense Stefan might have said that at least Van Damme (1) had a great butt, and (2) didn't need anyone to do his dirty work for him.

"But it's worse," Stefan said, returning to the conversation with his agent. "He may have to drop me, since I'm not bringing in much money now."

"What? Agents don't drop clients—it's supposed to be the other way around."

Right then in the kitchen, with Stefan brooding and gloomy, I decided, what the hell, I'd eat some cheese puffs and have some wine—it wouldn't kill me, and it might cheer him up. Hell, I'd empty the bottle with him if it helped. I certainly would be able to stomach the dean's reception a little better if I were buzzed.

But before I could announce my intention, Stefan said, "Maybe I should just give up completely, and stop writing books, just teach my classes—"

"—and live with blinders on? You've always been a writer—that's not just what you do, it's who you are. You can't just stop, turn it off like a faucet."

Stefan rose to check the gougères, each movement heavy

and sad. I wanted again to suggest that he go into therapy, but the very last time I had said it, he had leaned into my face and said very sharply, "I don't need a shrink—I need success."

I tried to rally him by changing the subject. "You're not going to believe who's in the basement with me."

Stefan frowned. "What? Who?"

"At Parker. Byron Summerscale's been assigned to EAR, and they've put him down in the basement—in a supply closet."

"Nick, you're making that up."

"Not a word. It's all true. I joke about my office, but his really was a supply closet. They cleaned it out, but just barely—and they left the sign outside over the door. It's grotesque. No window, barely any room to breathe when he closes the door. I'd go nuts in there." I took Stefan through my Surround Sound encounter with Summerscale, making it even funnier than it had been originally, but Stefan smiled only fitfully. Damn—and I was working so hard at it.

"They want him to quit," he concluded.

"Duh. But he said he's going to bring the whole fucking school down around their heads."

"Nick—"

"I am not exaggerating. He thinks he's Samson tied to the pillars of the temple. Well, he does have the hair for it. They're so vicious they were ready to assign him to limbo, to the dean's office, and have him do nothing but get his paycheck anyway. This stuff is too crazy to invent. Why aren't you writing any of it down? Your agent's an idiot to suggest writing a thriller. You should be updating Kingsley Amis and David Lodge."

"Oh, that would great," he sneered. "Academic satire? Who cares?"

"It worked for Jane Smiley," I said, even though I'd found *Moo* obvious and too long; I preferred her short stories and her novellas, and anyway Laurie Colwin had always struck me as a stronger writer.

"That's because she was Jane Smiley," Stefan said. "She could have written any kind of book and it would have been a hit after *A Thousand Acres* and a Pulitzer."

"Hey, that sounds good, way better than forty acres and a mule."

Stefan shook his head.

Annoyed that my Summerscale anecdote hadn't interested him much, I tried again before Stefan could start griping about Smiley and best-seller lists. "Okay, guess who was at the pool?" I must have sounded like a mother trying to jolly her flu-bedraggled child.

Stefan gamely asked who.

"Dean Bullerschmidt!"

Now he cracked a real smile. "The dean can *swim?*" He blinked his eyes rapidly, as if trying to absorb the thought.

"No way. He was water-walking—and it was grisly, like a forced march." I went on to embellish that description, leaving Juno out of the story. "And you wouldn't believe his body. Folds and pouches of fat, like the Hanging Gardens of Babylon or something. Layers—tiers—terraces! And he has—I'm not kidding—he has *tits*—flabby, flat, wrinkled, hairy tits. It was disgusting. I know I'm being body-ist," I said with mock solemnity, "but honestly, it could have been the opening of *Scream* 3."

Stefan smiled at my rhetorical excesses.

"So you know what I was thinking?" I continued. "You know how after-dinner speakers will tell you that when you're intimidated by someone, you should try imagining them in the buff? Well, now we can. Isn't that great?"

This quip didn't amuse Stefan at all—it had the opposite effect.

"The reception," he muttered. "Camille."

Shit, I thought, we were never going to hear the end of his griping about her. "Listen, Stefan, I bet even Camille has had crummy times in her career, and lousy reviews, and bad sales figures too."

"Sure—but look where she is now."

Well, how could anyone dispute that? Camille had landed like Dorothy's farmhouse right in the middle of Oz, and Stefan felt like the crushed Wicked Witch. The party for Cypriani had obviously been buzzing at him for days.

"When they hired *me*," he said, "there wasn't a reception at the dean's house, it was in the damned Union."

Of course, Stefan had never won a Pulitzer, nor had he been chosen for an endowed chair, but reminding him of that would have been cruel.

"I'm not going tonight. I want to stay home."

I did not ask if he planned to watch *Sudden Death* for the eighteenth time.

"Stefan, you're always telling me I have to be careful about what I say in EAR. You chewed my head off for making that crack about burning the Jurevicius Library books at Homecoming, remember? You told me it might backfire on me somehow?"

He nodded dolefully.

"Well, if you don't go to the reception, it's tantamount to a very public comment you cannot afford to make—that's simply not an option. If you don't go, Camille might not give a shit, but Serena will, and you don't know who else you'll offend."

"Probably Bullerschmidt," he grumbled.

"That's right, Bullerschmidt." The rumor mill said that Cypriani had the full support of our ponderous and brutal dean, though some people claimed it was because of his generally meek, submissive wife Nina. She was rumored to be a fervent reader of Cypriani's novels. "Stefan, you're the writer-in-residence, and you have to show up, and you have to be nice to Camille Cypriani even if you'd love to see her crash in a helicopter like that terrorist guy trying to kill Van Damme."

Stefan grinned beatifically at the image. "That would be a great way for her to die."

"At this point," I said, "any way would be a great way for her to die—as long as it's quick. But I don't think we're going to be lucky. She may drink like Faulkner and smoke like Winston Churchill, but from everything I've seen and heard, Camille is mean, bone mean, and people like that live forever."

The timer buzzed for the first wave of gougères. Stefan perked up, pulled out the tray to let them cool, and prepared another batch to go in. When we finally sampled them and poured ourselves some wine, and he was asking me to replay some of

Summerscale's outrageous lines, which I was inventing freely by then, I decided this was most definitely not the right time to tell Stefan about the Dante prank, or the flyer.

Stefan did some laundry in the afternoon, while I tried not to feel too aggrieved that he hadn't really asked me about my day and meant it, or even responded much when I tried describing my Theater of Cruelty encounters with Bullerschmidt and Summerscale. But I was equally conscious of having skipped a full or accurate description of my time with Juno, in and out of the pool. As for what she had unexpectedly stirred in me, or made me open up to—

I was not used to hiding something so important from Stefan, though once before I had briefly but seriously wondered about Stefan's involvement in a murder, because he'd revealed a connection with the victim I hadn't known about. This morning's interlude with Juno was different, but just as threatening. Maybe more so. As T. S. Eliot wrote in *The Cocktail Party*, "What we know of other people/Is only our memory of the moments/During which we knew them," and so in a way I could accept Stefan's ultimate unknowableness to me. But contemplating something so alien and secret in myself was far more alarming.

I spent the rest of the afternoon before the reception for Camille Cypriani out in the sun room, reading a superb biography of Georges Simenon, *The Man Who Wasn't Maigret*.

5

S we drove off in Stefan's Volvo to Dean Bullerschmidt's reception, I told Stefan that he looked great, and he did. But I was also worried that he'd been spending a lot of money on clothes lately. His new suede shirt cost $650—was he blowing big bucks on clothes to make himself feel better? If so, it wasn't working. I had hinted at therapy, or even just trying some St. John's Wort, but Stefan hadn't responded well.

"I did therapy years ago," he said.

"Then think of this as a booster shot."

"Give him some time," Sharon had said to me wryly. "Joseph Abboud and Jhane Barnes make great men's clothes—that could work." And over my demurral, she said, "Sweetie, with so many things to fret about, you're worried that Stefan looks so good? Honey, if he'd been taller, he could have been a model. Just enjoy it—the money's coming from his business account, anyway, right, and not your joint account?"

"Well, what if he's audited? What if he's thrown into jail for tax fraud or something? Hot clothes aren't a business expense unless you're a call boy."

There wasn't a dire fantasy of mine Sharon had ever been flummoxed by. Now she laughed. "Okay. Then we'll visit him in jail, and he'll have heartbreaking material for a book. Or you will."

Dean Bullerschmidt lived in a huge gloomy home in one of Michiganapolis's pricier neighborhoods, Michigan Estates, due north of us. This community was studded with oversize, extravagantly landscaped homes, many of them worth over half a million dollars, which was a lot in Michiganapolis.

Dozens of cars lined his street on either side of the large, hulking house with its deep overhang, ominously glossy white bricks, and huge, carved, dark double doors. Darth Vader's summer cottage.

We'd been there only once before, under very awkward circumstances, so it was definitely an unpleasant return for me, but more so for Stefan. Our knock was answered by a uniformed hired flunky, probably some local "yute" (as Joe Pesci calls them in *My Cousin Vinny*), and the noise inside hit us like a wave of summer heat when you step out of an air-conditioned mall.

Stefan was instantly jealous as he pointed out to me the exquisite flower arrangements in the marble-floored hall—dendrobium orchids, Stargazer lilies, double pink lisianthus that looked like old-fashioned roses, and white mini carnations. In the cherry-paneled dining room to our right, Chinese-style vases filled with lavender-blue roses and misty blue limonium studded the giant buffet tablet.

"This is costing a fortune," he muttered, eyeing the lavish buffet as we approached through the crowd. He blanched when he saw the serried ranks of champagne bottles. And every food item on the long damask-draped table had been tormented into the resemblance of something else: there were pâté sailing ships, shrimp frogs, castles of crudités, and so on. Glancing around me, I couldn't help agree with Stefan's continued quiet complaints, even as I took a glass of Veuve Clicquot for myself.

Stefan wandered off, probably to take an insulting inventory of the party's delights, while I stood back to watch the faculty enjoying unaccustomed goodies in an extremely plush setting.

For the most part, EAR department and even college functions didn't usually go beyond boxed wine and prepared cheese dips.

As I took it all in, able to see several rooms from my vantage point, it amused me to realize that the party was markedly segregated. Former Rhetoric Department professors had congregated in the gleaming stainless steel and white-on-white kitchen off the dining room, where I could see a busy catering staff dashing around them with annoyance. They were probably trying to chat up the staff because they felt out of their depth in Bullerschmidt's Ralph Lauren Home Collection-ish house. I thought of my Belgian-born mother quietly mocking Americans: "You all try to make friends with your waiters. *C'est pas digne*—it's not dignified. I don't want a new friend when I go out to eat, I want a well-presented, good meal. A waiter should be a professional, not a confidant."

My hanging back that night and studying the crowd was kind of funny, since I'd always been so extroverted, while it was Stefan who tended to silent observation in groups. I wondered if after fifteen years together we hadn't started to pick up each other's habits. Not exactly like a dog and his owner coming to resemble each other—but close.

Across the hall, Camille Cypriani, Dean Bullerschmidt, SUM's lame-brained President Littleterry, Provost Coral Greathouse, and other SUM bigwigs were encamped in the dean's library with all the gravitas of a think tank running a symposium about the effect of global warming on the Euro. I suppose, to be polite, I should have gone over to the dean and his wife to thank them for inviting me and Stefan, but I didn't feel like it. I listened to the music coming from somewhere, and after a few minutes I realized it was Beethoven's Sixth Piano Concerto, the transcription he'd done himself of his violin concerto. I wondered if that was a deliberate choice, if the dean had chosen this rarely played piece so that he could flummox guests who thought there were only five Beethoven concertos for piano. That is, if anyone had the nerve to ask.

Lesser faculty from the College of Arts and Letters, many of whom seemed a bit dazed to have been invited, were circulating nervously from room to room, as if agitated by the bright lights, the sense of privilege. About a dozen of the department's adjunct and gypsy scholars squatted miserably on the staircase up to some kind of loft, looking decidedly rootless and uncomfortable and muttering about the cost of this event. I nodded their way, but hardly knew any of them because they weren't at Parker Hall often enough. I edged closer to listen to them gripe about the party, but tried to keep my stance of neutral party-goer quietly taking in the scene.

One of them said this kind of reception was taking away from higher salaries they could be earning. "Dream on," I thought.

Dressed all in charcoal gray, Cash Jurevicius sat in the center of this envy-ridden assemblage, seeming to hold court. There was a smoldering air about him of someone very powerful keeping his violence under tight control—a Ninja Adjunct. His pretty face with its surfer boy curls was red from booze or anger—or both. In a low voice as resonant and cultivated as a public radio announcer's, he said, "Older professors should step aside before retirement and let new blood have a chance."

Jeez, where had I heard something like that before? There was somebody young complaining about not getting a chance —but where? In a movie? And which one?

Cash scowled. "I can't believe they gave an endowed chair to Camille Cypriani. She's not a writer, she's a book machine, and she's been coasting on her Pulitzer for years."

I wasn't sure he was wrong. The editor of *The Godfather* once said that the problem with publishing was that all the people who had half a mind to write a book, did so.

Cash waved me over, but I hesitated. He was starting to seem as quietly challenging as Albee's George and Martha, and I had no plans of playing "Get the Guest" tonight, right out there in the entryway.

"Don't you agree?" he called. "Isn't EAR full of deadwood? They need a forest fire to clear it all out—or a few sharp axes." Eyes around him glinted with malicious amusement at this assessment—and to see me put on the spot. Everyone knew I was untenured, and even if I agreed, I couldn't say so publicly. So the game was in seeing how much I'd equivocate.

I moved closer. "All universities are alike," I said, trying for a global assessment. "You can't change how they operate." Even if someone important were eavesdropping, there wasn't anything too damning in what I'd said.

Cash grinned. "Every empire crumbles eventually," he said, and I thought he couldn't be too drunk if he brought out that near-tongue-twister so cleanly.

"Look what Gandhi did in India," someone on the stairs piped up, and there was a wave of drunken giggling in Cash's audience.

Cash rubbed his hands together thoughtfully. "EAR is beyond nonviolence," he said oracularly, to appreciative murmuring, and I wondered if they were planning to make pipe bombs after the reception.

I decided to leave Cash to his prognostications and his fan club. Even though Cash was no better off than the other temporaries, he had an air of privilege because he carried himself like the pretender to the throne. He might not have had any power, but his grandmother once had, as chair of EAR, and some of it seemed to linger about him. No wonder he was surrounded and admired.

As I headed off, bland Carter Savery and irate and wiry Iris Bell walked past, heads bent toward each other, whispering angrily. I watched them find a corner of the dining room, where they appeared to be locked in some kind of argument. Like other former Rhetoric faculty, they seemed dissatisfied not just with their years-old amalgamation into the larger department, their status in EAR, and the courses they taught, but with life itself.

I'd heard various stories about them: for instance, that Carter had been a superb tennis player but broke a wrist in a car accident and had to give it up. Likewise, Iris had always wanted to be a novelist, so it was said, but never managed to publish. These faculty perpetually reminded me of Brando's complaint in *On the Waterfront* that he "coulda been somebody" but in their case, I wasn't so sure.

I assumed that for both Iris and Carter, teaching was not their first love. So watching Camille Cypriani swan about the department with the kind of money, influence, and fame that had eluded them must have been maddening—and if Stefan was upset by this lavish reception, they were even more incensed. So much hostility in this house. Was the person who targeted me with the flyer and the book here tonight, feeding on that negativity? Watching me, observing me to see if I was rattled, smirkingly planning something else, something harsher? Was it crazy to wonder if this was only the beginning, if I was going to be stalked?

I had heard people talk about feeling "a presence" in a haunted room or house. Well, that's what I felt now, and it was definitely malicious.

From my spot not far from the front door, I watched the dean lumberingly avoid standing too close to Coral Greathouse every time the crowd around them shifted. She was his former rival for the job of provost, but he had to at least pretend civility toward her. But Camille Cypriani, either drunk or sullen or both, was an even more diverting spectacle. She dismissed anyone trying to seek an audience with her, as if the administrators' circle was the only acceptable company for her (though she wasn't exactly Chatty Cathy with those folks, either).

Cypriani, a Peggy Lee look-alike with a librarian's bun and a purple chiffon pantsuit, had a disdainful, almost reptilian stare that seemed to dare people to be interesting enough to ignore. I was fascinated by her, and repulsed, as I drifted closer to where she glowered and weaved a bit. She'd be "so easy to hate," I thought, inverting the Gershwin song.

Something had apparently kick-started Cypriani, because I could hear her loudly telling some anecdote about being on tour in Hungary. Thus far, when she was voluble, it seemed to be only about herself. "They adore me like the Hapsburgs there," she said in her gravelly voice. "I was besieged. There was this charming and devoted fan—a count, of course—who appeared at my rather luxurious hotel—the publisher spoiled me, but then they always do—with two beautiful valises, just beautiful, filled with copies of my books he begged me to sign." Nods and smiles of various levels of sycophancy greeted this story and continued through its self-deluded banalities, though it seemed clear to me that only Nina Bullerschmidt was really attentive, and she had the stifled rapt look of a young peasant girl who'd just seen the Blessed Virgin appear in her milk pail.

I turned from this distasteful spectacle and wandered into the baronial kitchen with a skylighted breakfast room that looked like one of those fantasies on HGTV: culinary porn. Catering staffers were rushing about, weaving in and out of the faculty, who ignored their haste and need for room. The whole atmosphere was too frantic for me, so I headed out the other entrance to the kitchen, passing a pantry as large as our own kitchen. Someone must have taken off the rear wall of the house in remodeling to create that much space.

Back in the thick of things I was surprised that Juno Dromgoole, dressed in a floor-length tight black skirt and partly sheer glittery leopard-print blouse, with her dark blond hair resplendently spiky, was chatting quite amiably with Serena Fisch. Heavily made-up Serena looked striking as usual in a retro violet, sequin-trimmed coatdress—a kabuki Joan Crawford.

Juno looked really hot, and I watched her for a moment, picturing her back in the pool, flushed and wet and breathing hard. What would it be like to run my hands and tongue down her neck onto her breasts and bury my face between them? I tried to stifle the image.

Juno and Serena—were they still friends? Then perhaps Juno hadn't told anyone but me yet that she was planning to run for chair. When the news got out, though, there was going to be chaos. Juno might not have been popular, but I could imagine a strong anti-Rhetoric faculty vote, so she could win out of spite, which would further embitter a mean-spirited department.

My attention was drawn back to Cypriani holding court. I'd only seen Nina Bullerschmidt a few times, and though well—and expensively—dressed, she generally had the kind of hangdog look of betrayed trailer trash on the *Ricki Lake Show*. But tonight she seemed almost feverishly composed and happy.

Her back was straighter, and her face was flushed as she hovered around Cypriani, bringing her drinks, handing her a scalloped silver ashtray, intervening between her and the waiters passing through the house with hors d'oeuvres as if she were Cypriani's personal assistant. Nobody seemed at all surprised by this excessive solicitousness, least of all Dean Bullerschmidt, who seemed from time to time otiosely benevolent, as if he'd somehow created not just the endowed chair but Cypriani herself.

Dashing past me now to the kitchen, Nina stopped, turned to me, and gushed, "Lord, she's wonderful! She's a genius! Reading her books changed my life. I could read any one of them a hundred times. There's nobody else worth reading today. It's a crime that she hasn't won the Nobel Prize! And think, SUM's got her!" Then she was off.

I was amazed by this outpouring, which suggested there was much more to Nina Bullerschmidt than I had ever imagined. It fascinated me to see such a meek woman come alive—and about literature, too. Was it possible that Nina's passion for Cypriani's fiction was what led to her getting the chair, with Nina influencing the decision through Dean Bullerschmidt? And this question led to other reflections about the dean and Nina, making me wonder if it was at all possible that I'd been too quick to judge the saurian dean. But then I flip-flopped and considered whether there wasn't something a little creepy and false about Nina's enthusiasm.

Suddenly I flashed on Anne Baxter sucking up to Bette Davis in *All About Eve*, and Davis musing "Eve Evil, Little Miss Evil." Could there be something quietly malevolent in Nina's attentions to Cypriani? What the hell could she be up to? And where was Stefan? I needed him to tell me whether I was already so jaded by being at SUM that even when someone was nice, it seemed suspicious. I realized it was a scene in that movie Cash had just reminded me of, when Anne Baxter is quoted as decrying the theater's dominance by older actresses who wouldn't move on.

I snagged another glass of champagne from a nondescript

passing waiter, whose pants were so tight I could tell he wasn't wearing underwear, though he was the kind of guy who needed a lot of support. He caught me staring and grinned invitingly before drifting off. Well, once again I had reassuring proof that I hadn't undergone some kind of sea change in the pool with Juno. I wasn't completely lost—I still recognized my own internal landmarks.

But I was too full of gougères to try any of the expensive snacks, and so I wandered off into a cozy home theater furnished with a Turkish kilim and large club chairs where the solitary bookcase was crammed with Camille Cypriani's novels. Though I wasn't very familiar with her oeuvre, I counted seventeen novels. Not just the hardcover editons, either—they jostled with the trade and mass market paperbacks, as well as foreign editions and even advanced reader's copies. This was one serious collection.

Just as I was about to slip a book from its shelf to see if it was a signed first edition, I heard Camille passing by, snarling, "People are morons—they believe what they see—they believe what you tell them."

I poked my head out and caught Camille hustling Coral Greathouse down the hallway. What was that about, and why did she sound so angry? I drew back, but before I could even consider it further and wonder what they were talking about, Iris Bell and Carter Savery barged in, waving at the bookshelves, which they apparently had seen before, perhaps even studied.

"It's criminal," they both said, railing at the unfairness of someone like Cypriani, who was already rich, garnering such a huge salary "to do nothing!"

"All year she just has to stand around and be literary," Iris whined.

"She's actually doing a lot," I pointed out. "She's terrific window dressing for the university—she's a high-profile writer. She's been in *People* and lots of women's magazines, so she's somebody who can put a more popular face on SUM. Too bad she's not a minority or disabled, but she's still damned good PR for SUM."

Iris and Carter exchanged confused, angry glances.

"But what SUM really needs is to go hip-hop," I continued. "Then we could get on MTV and really make a difference. I mean, who needs those dumb black robes at graduation? Gold chains, backward baseball caps, tattoos, ski parkas, and baggy pants—that's the wave of the future. And we could get Puff Daddy as graduation speaker, or Lauryn Hill, or Snoop—" I filled their simmering silence with a quiet, "Just kidding."

Iris and Carter turned from me to stare at Cypriani's books with undisguised loathing, as if they'd completely missed my last remarks. I would not have been surprised if they'd started ripping them from the shelves, stomping on them, tearing them apart, and even pissing on them.

"You like her work?" Iris demanded of me. "You like her? You think she belongs here?" Iris's elfin face was twisted with venom. "Anyone could write the bilge that Cypriani's churned out for years. Even *I* could, if I hadn't been stuck grading composition papers year after year after year, with no chance of getting a novel published." Carter patted her meager shoulder sympathetically.

God, I thought, Iris wasn't just a frustrated writer, she was the kind of amateur who stupidly thought that writing only took some free time.

"And she won a Pulitzer?" Iris sneered.

"Well, Pulitzers are notoriously political. Edith Wharton won hers because the committee didn't want to give it to Sinclair Lewis that year."

Carter and Iris seemed to enjoy that bit of news. They were even more mollified when I decided to answer Iris's angry questions about how I felt about Cypriani and her work.

"I would never have agreed to bringing Cypriani to SUM." That was more about Stefan than Cypriani, but Iris and Carter didn't need an explanation. "Not that anyone in EAR or anywhere else in the university was consulted, as far as we know," I added. "And now there are all these people who'd like to pull that endowed chair right out from under her," I quipped, feeling nervous and guilty for being mildly dishonest with them—but what else could I do when these two individuals would be the ones making the decision about my tenure review?

Savery and Bell were quite pleased by my apparent solidarity, and they conspiratorially said they were counting on me, but left without saying what they meant by that or what they were planning. Great, I thought, Carter and Iris are plotting a revolution, and they probably expect me to do the academic equivalent of running a blockade. Couldn't I just sit by the guillotine and knit?

But I didn't panic; I was amused to see that Iris and Carter headed straight for Camille, out in the hallway. She smiled disdainfully at them in what appeared to be a suck-up session. Unbelievable! They had just been trashing her, and now they were buzzing around her only slightly less solicitously than Nina Bullerschmidt. Well, it was probably not a bad idea, since Camille was EAR's new power center, and if they couldn't somehow get rid of her or undermine her, they might as well score some points.

I settled into a comfortable club chair, content to sip champagne and let the party go on around me, musing on how even the evening Bullerschmidt chose for the reception was a sign of the dean's typical bullishness: a Monday night. This made it harder for people to deal with Tuesday classes, whether they'd be hung over or simply have stayed out too late, but obviously the dean didn't care. He was a workaholic and totally unsympathetic to anyone whose standards he deemed lower.

Stefan mooched in, confessing that he had been avoiding Camille, and that he'd counted the bottles of champagne. "It's Bollinger and Veuve Cliquot," he griped. "Where'd all the money come from for this lousy party?"

"Stefan, administrators on campus can produce funds for anything they want whenever they want, you know that. This bacchanal is chicken feed in their scheme of things." I reminded him of the studies we'd read that showed SUM was not just top-heavy with administrators, but perhaps one of the worst offenders in this way in the Midwest. "That's the way things are."

But just as I was about to warn Stefan to get a grip on himself and stop complaining, Coral Greathouse strolled in, looking rather severe in low heels and one of her typical badly cut brownish ex-nun suits and low heels. She hadn't changed her stony demeanor, drab style, or red Sally Jesse Raphael glasses since she'd become provost, but I felt a difference nonetheless. Her powerful position had made her even more reserved, more self-contained.

I was chilled when she said, "Nick, I wanted to tell you something."

I waited anxiously.

"I do hope that you'll keep out of trouble as your application for promotion and tenure moves forward. It's important that people think well of you," she said flatly. "It's important that people *speak* well of you."

Coral Greathouse was the one who made the final decision after reviewing the tenure committee's findings, and she could overrule whatever decision reached her from EAR, so I assumed she meant it was important that *she* thought well of me. I felt as if Coral had sought me out because she thought I was misbehaving somehow, and I had the absurd urge to yell like a little kid, "I wasn't doing anything! Honest!"

Instead, I just thanked her for the advice, and she left us alone, without once having acknowledged Stefan's presence in the room. It was as if she had come to deliver a message from the Mob, and nobody else's presence mattered.

I'd broken out in a sweat and wiped my face with the cocktail napkin from my drink.

Stefan was shaking his head. "Coral can do whatever she wants to at SUM," he marveled. "She controls everything." He sounded wistful, tired, and envious.

Juno suddenly whirled into the room, red-faced. "That bloody bitch! She deserves to die!"

6

I ALMOST spilled my champagne at the phrase, so close to what had been written on the flyer. Was the choice of words coincidental, or an unconscious slip? If not, then Juno was playing some sick game with me, teasing me, leading me on, and trashing me. Could she be a split personality? No, that was unlikely—Juno's personality was so outrageous, there wasn't any room left over in her for another.

Juno barreled on, cursing, stalking back and forth. If she'd had a cigarette in her hand, she would probably have set something on fire. Vibrant, incensed, self-dramatizing, she reminded me of Bette Davis in *All About Eve* when she discovers that Eve Harrington had been her secret understudy and had taken her place at a reading. But I did not think I should make the comparison for her. Boy, that movie was buzzing around in my head like the last song you hear on the radio in the morning.

"I tried chatting Camille up, but I might as well adopt a Tasmanian devil as a house pet! Talking to her is like pissing up a cliff! I told her about having lunch with Margaret Atwood last month and how Atwood remarked that she admired the ending of Camille's last book. And do you know what that wench said?"

Stefan sat on the wide arm of my chair, and together we asked, "What?"

Juno stopped pacing and stood with her legs slightly spread as if she were a contralto bracing herself for an aria of malediction. "She said she didn't read Atwood because she avoided provincial writers! That Canada was simply too young a country to have produced anything worth the name of literature! Can you believe her balls?"

Juno looked angry enough to ram one of Atwood's or even one of her own books down Cypriani's throat. Suddenly she grinned and, eyebrows waggling, crowed with delight, "Camille may think she's a class act, but she doesn't even know the right way to hold a champagne glass. She's holding it by the bowl, not the stem!"

I tried lightening the mood further. "Martha Stewart would really approve of your attention to detail." But Juno's face darkened, and she stalked from the room with this comment: "I'd strangle that high and mighty bitch if she were worth the effort."

Stefan and I looked at each other as if we'd been through a storm-caused power outage and the lights had just flickered back on. Grimly, he said, "We're going to be having more encounters like that one to look forward to."

"True. Camille's making enemies faster than Judge Starr hands down indictments."

Stefan took my glass and finished the champagne, setting it down on a nearby marble-topped table. Watching him, I felt embarrassed to be suddenly imagining Juno flushed and vocal in more intimate circumstances. And pouring champagne from a glass down her breasts and licking them dry.

Jeez, was I a closet heterosexual?

Before I could follow that thought, there was a sound of glasses crashing out in the hall, and we rushed out to find a waiter on the floor, apparently having collided with Byron Summerscale, who was squinting and apparently dead drunk. People crowded close to see what was going on while Nina and the rest of the catering staff apologetically tried to clean up the mess with napkins and little brooms, but didn't get very far because Byron lay there unmoving and unmovable.

I shuddered. The large, tangled crowd and the body on the floor reminded me of last spring's horrible incident on the Administration Building bridge, and I suddenly felt dizzy. Stefan picked up on it instantly and slid an arm around me to keep me steady. He squeezed me until I felt solid and then let me go, without saying anything. And this was the man I was betraying in my thoughts—a man who picked up what I was feeling and comforted me immediately? How could I be so ungrateful—and obsessed? Obsession was no hyperbole—I was thinking about Juno more than I'd ever thought of any woman before, and far more intimately.

President Littleterry stormed over to the recumbent Summerscale. Grizzled and weather-beaten, SUM's ex–football coach and current president had spent decades shouting at players, referees, and judges during games, so his face was permanently fixed in an expression of fierce discontent. Now he looked especially disgusted, ready to chew Summerscale a new asshole.

"You're drunk—you're a disgrace—get the hell out of here," the president began, but ursine Summerscale staggered heavily to his feet, towering over Littleterry. If he'd smashed his head in with one big paw, I don't think any of us would have been surprised.

"*I'm* a disgrace? You're the one turning this university into a sick joke!" He pointed a sausage-fat finger at him and thundered, "You're a disgrace!" as if he were Satan himself carting Don Juan off to hell in *Don Giovanni*.

There were gasps from the crowd, but Summerscale wasn't done by any means. "You're a thug—an assassin. You're killing everything good and true at this university—it's all one big cash register to you, and public relations."

Juno sidled over to me and murmured, "Isn't this marvelous, it's like an opera," and I wasn't just hyperaware of her perfume and her body heat, but also of her being on the same wavelength as I was. In response to my deep and appreciative breathing, Juno identified what she was wearing as Eternity. Stefan was oblivious to this byplay, but I started to blush.

Littleterry balled his fists and pounded on his chest as if about to give a Tarzan yell. "You're a goddamned drunk," he shouted.

"And you're an anti-intellectual moron."

"Has-been limpdick."

"Churl! Visigoth!"

This name-calling escalated (or degenerated, depending on your perspective) until Littleterry mocked Summerscale's late department as "lousy with faggots and commies and wimps." Summerscale upped the ante by deriding the president's former coaching skills. This was too much for the president, whose face purpled: "You're nuts!" he cried. "We went to the Rose Bowl!"

"It was just dumb luck—you sucked, only everyone else sucked worse that year. If Ohio State had a better offense, you'd have been dead."

There were quiet nods of agreement among those in the crowd who followed the team.

Littleterry lunged at Summerscale, who stiff-armed him as if he were John Elway at the Super Bowl. People started laughing. Summerscale suddenly let go, and the president fell. There was no laughter now. Bullerschmidt, Greathouse, and other administrators rushed to help the president to his feet, but he furiously waved them off, glaring at Summerscale, who started to make a moderately dignified exit.

It was a bizarre and exciting scene; here for the first time was someone publicly saying what many people at SUM thought—and directly to those in power. So there was a vicarious thrill for most of us that night watching Littleterry get mau-maued. But it was also scary; even people in the room who would have liked to egg Summerscale on dreaded what might happen to him or anyone who challenged SUM authority.

"If this were a bar," Littleterry roared, "you'd be tossed out on your can."

"It's close," Summerscale said as he slipped out the front door. "It's a whorehouse."

There was complete silence, and Stefan and I nervously drew closer together, as if we were about to witness Hamlet stab Polonius through the arras in his mother's bedroom, but Littleterry didn't react.

Nina Bullerschmidt tactfully announced dessert, and there was a general sugartropic move away from scandal toward the buffet table, now seductively laden with multitiered trays of sweets. We followed, and I was impressed by the trifle, tiramisù, Linzer tarts, brownies, Russian tea cakes, Pavlova, and macaroons. Stefan dolefully surveyed the caloric cornucopia while I distractedly wondered what it would be like to feed Juno a brownie or a macaroon, piece by piece. . . .

I studied Bullerschmidt, who seemed upset about more than the gross breach of decorum and the assault on the president's and SUM's dignity. The dean's face was creased with anxiety or doubt, and he was watching Nina suspiciously. I whispered to Stefan, "What if that scene wasn't really about the university—what if Summerscale's having an affair with Littleterry's wife, and that's why she's not here?"

"She's not here because she's dead. She's been dead for years, remember? She got crushed by that Homecoming float."

"Well, maybe Nina's coked up, maybe that's why she's so uncharacteristically ebullient."

"What?"

"Or maybe she's a lesbian and infatuated with Cypriani."

"You think everyone's gay," Stefan snapped, and then apologized for being so sour. "That's not remotely true," he added. "I don't know why I even said it."

Well, I did; Stefan was upset and had to lash out at somebody, but understanding that didn't make it feel any better. Stung by Stefan's moodiness, I ploughed somewhat too heartily into dessert, but couldn't take much delight in what I was scarfing down.

Suddenly President Littleterry was clinking a glass in the dining room, showing no signs of outrage at the recent fracas.

He held his champagne glass—the "wrong way," I noticed—and tapped it with a silver knife as if he were at a wedding, then handed the knife to a startled waiter.

"Gather round," he called, and I winced at his corniness. Littleterry smacked at and dug into his pockets with his free hand, apparently looking for a speech, but couldn't find anything and probably decided to wing it. There was general nervousness in the room; our nitwit president was not known as being swift of tongue, even when well coached by his overpaid minions.

He began as sententiously as if he were commemorating some famous battle, or Eliza Doolittle making sure she got her vowels right: "We are here tonight to honor the seat that has been given to Camille Cypriani."

I winced at his choice of words, and could feel part of my brain drifting off to sleep. Juno had moved over to my side, and she whispered mockingly: "Seat? She's not a fucking senator."

Littleterry went on to give a short speech that was equal parts incoherence and ignorance, and briefly I wondered if Summerscale might have swiped the president's speech in their fracas. There were obligatory references to SUM as a great institution and Michigan as a great state, along with slams of the University of Michigan. Most people at SUM could have easily spun those weak filaments together into a speech, but even this simple rhetorical embroidery was beyond Littleterry. He kept coughing, saying "uh—," and glancing around the room as if expecting to be rescued. His face exhibited a Nixonian sheen.

"The man gives village idiots a bad name," Juno muttered.

It was apparent not only that the president was very uncomfortable speaking without a prepared text, but worse, that he had very little idea who exactly Cypriani was. He even mispronounced her first and second names more than once. Littleterry also mentioned her books randomly, leaving out the Pulitzer winner, and he never even looked at her or gestured her way as you might expect him to do.

During the whole embarrassing scene, Juno kept up a consistent chorus of murmured ridicule, making me feel like I was sitting with the class clown in junior high and desperately trying not to crack up. Stefan didn't seem to be tuned in to any of this, whether because he'd disappeared into his own psychic wormhole or because he'd had too much champagne, I didn't know. But I was actually relieved that Stefan's awareness of what was going on around him—at least right then—was so dim.

Littleterry suddenly, awkwardly shifted gears just at the point I expected him to introduce Cypriani to general applause. He announced, "I now want to speak about presenting a Bold New Initiative that will take SUM into the Twentieth Century—and Beyond."

"Twenty-*first*," Bullerschmidt rumbled from across the room. "Twenty-first century."

Littleterry beamed: "Exactly!" And he paused dramatically, holding up his empty champagne glass as if about to make a toast. He blathered about the millennium, progress, responsibility, great changes, and the like.

Camille Cypriani's face had hardened. Not surprisingly, she was pissed off to no longer be the center of even muddled attention and to have been shunted aside by this mysterious news. Almost everyone else at the party looked puzzled or annoyed, and whispers flared up like fireplace flames licking the edge of a log. All that champagne followed by all that sugar had made people a bit woozy, but we were wary, too, given the president's history.

Littleterry had previously advocated doing more with less under the rubric of "High IQ" (Improving Quality), a project that basically suggested replacing live professors with taped television classes. Then there was NAME (New Associates Making Excellence), which involved renaming professors as "learning associates," administrators as "management associates," secretaries and other support staff as "operational associates," and students as "guests." Neither plan went anywhere despite the ballyhoo and mountains of paperwork and press releases, so there was clear trepidation about what he was about to spring on this assembly. Whatever it was would doubtless involve a great deal of wasted effort. This was, after all, a university devoted to "strategic planning," which meant (1) get as many people involved to give the administration feedback; (2) make them think their opinions matter; (3) get them to issue a massive report; and (4) do what you planned to do all along after thanking them for their time.

"In response to customer demand," Littleterry finally said portentously, "I am launching a task force to study the institution of a cutting-edge brand new program."

"As opposed to an *old* cutting-edge program," Juno drawled softly, just for me.

Of course, given all the budget cuts at SUM, this news was stunning, and Littleterry seemed to gloat at the attention and his power to command it, his smile an unspoken "Impressive, huh?"

Stefan turned to me and quoted our favorite party getaway lines from *Laura*: "I cannot stand these morons any longer. If you don't come with me this instant I shall run amok." I didn't argue. I nodded good night to Juno, and we threaded our way through the throngs of curious academics to the door. But before we reached it, we heard Littleterry announce that he was urging the foundation of a "Department of White Studies."

Stefan and I whirled around, and I'm sure if anyone had caught us on film, we would have been slack-jawed.

"It's time," the president said, "that whites received the same critical study and scrutiny that other groups in this great and noble society have gotten."

The house erupted in a flurry of shocked comments and questions, some startled applause greeted by hissing, which in turn elicited catcalls. All the while, Dean Bullerschmidt bellowed, "Not White Studies, *Whiteness* Studies! *Whiteness* Studies!"

Stefan and I escaped this mess, passing Cash Jurevicius, who was outside, smoking. He nodded, and I wondered how much practice in front of a mirror it took to make a nod so quietly supercilious. "Summerscale should be careful about calling so much attention to himself," he said cryptically, and turned away when I asked what he meant.

Nearby, Iris and Carter were getting into a car, but Iris stopped when she saw me and bustled over. "For your own good," she said crisply, "you should stop hanging around Juno Dromgoole. That woman is a menace—and a whore!"

There wasn't any time for me to tell Iris to fuck off, because she dashed back to her car. Yet I felt my whole body vibrating with the fantasy of shouting at her, and the whole stinking university. It would have sealed my doom as far as tenure was concerned, but it would have been a cry of liberation.

Stefan and I walked to his car while I cursed having to always hold back because of needing tenure, and how I had to be nice to people like Iris because of her role in my tenure application. God, I felt tainted by her and Carter's hatred for Camille, for Juno—for the world. The whole EAR department, and SUM, was seething with as much resentment as a medieval crusade against heretics. Oh, there might not have been smoking ruins and eviscerated corpses left after they did their work, but it was close. And Iris and Carter were all too typical of EAR, and incapable of seeing how twisted they'd become.

But then something else occurred to me: was anyone picking up my attraction to Juno—or would it have been so unexpected that no one would notice?

I bitched about them as they drove past us, but none of this affected Stefan. I pulled out my keys for Stefan's car, and he didn't object when I opened the driver's-side door and got in. He slumped next to me, drained, depressed, more miserable than even this afternoon when he'd talked about giving up writing forever. On the short ride home, he asked, "Is Littleterry out of his mind?"

"No. Well, he may be, but this Whiteness Studies thing is for real. Not that I ever expected to see it at SUM."

"It's not a joke?"

"Whiteness Studies is the latest campus trend in the United States."

"No way."

"Way. It's got roots in the memoir craze, pop culture studies, antimulticulturalism. People are nuts for anything new, especially if it's extreme and controversial—kind of like the intellectual version of piercing."

"But Whiteness Studies is— What the hell is it?"

"Anything. Lots of things. You can include white trash performance art, Elvis sightings, *Bastard out of Carolina*, whatever. More low culture than high, but not necessarily. Probably paintings on velvet. I've seen books about it, conferences, journal articles." I laughed. "My favorite article title is 'Tonya Harding: Victim or Vamp?' "

"You're making that up," Stefan accused me.

"Not one word is phony. Not one. Trust me. I've been clipping articles on Whiteness Studies. I've got them at home if you're interested." They were in the file drawer where I kept folders on ominous developments, feeling I had to be prepared, sort of like that Doris Lessing character in *The Four-Gated City*. I figure that if the Romans had been this organized, they might have staved off all those Goths.

Wearily, Stefan said, "Everybody's nuts."

"Whiteness Studies is hot this year. Last year it was Porn Studies that was big, before that it was Queer Studies and Madonna Studies. Hey—wouldn't that make a cool interdisciplinary degree? The three of those?"

Stefan seemed miserably sober now, and amazed. "How could I have missed this crap?" He sat up straighter as we pulled into our driveway.

I didn't give him the obvious answer: he'd been so lost in despair about his career he could easily have missed a nuclear war, so what was a new act in the perpetual academic freak show?

Dreading more chaos at SUM and in the department, when we got home I said I was going right to bed even though it wasn't very late, but Stefan wanted to stay downstairs for a drink. Just as I was about to tell Stefan he'd probably had enough to drink that evening, the doorbell rang.

I went to see who it was: our Quebecois neighbor Didier Charbonneau from across the street, who said he'd seen our light on.

Stefan waved him in and poured him some single malt
—Glenwhatsit.

Bald and burly Didier was in his usual jeans and white
T-shirt, looking like James Dean's grandpa, and he settled down
comfortably on the living room couch as if he expected a long
night's booze-up.

Didier's wife, Lucille Mochtar, an EAR faculty member
with whom I'd been sharing my office on the third floor before I
had to leave it, was guest-teaching at Duke that semester.
Didier, a retired high school teacher, only visited her for week-
ends because he loathed anything south of Pennsylvania.
Lonely, he'd been hanging out even more than usual with
Stefan, his workout buddy at the Club. But they shared more
than weights now: Didier's much-heralded memoir about his in-
fertility was clearly doomed. In the wake of a conglomerate buying his publisher, a low laydown had led his publisher to cancel
a large tour and scrap the advertising campaign. Loud and usually cheerful Didier had fallen to pieces over the changing fortunes of his book, and wasn't exactly the most life-affirming
company Stefan could have right now. He too loathed Camille
Cypriani, as he would any writer who'd been a success.

I'd quickly grown tired of their contrapuntal whining and
wasn't interested in another evening's dose, not to mention the
obnoxious smoke from Didier's Kohiba, which he was readying,
so I left them downstairs. On the way to bed, I imagined what
Lucille Mochtar might say when she heard about the Whiteness
Studies initiative, since she was half black.

When I closed the bedroom door, I sighed with a sense of
ease. We'd bought a new bed over the summer—a romantic,
king-size, cherry sleigh bed—which meant all new sheets. We'd
chosen comforter and pillows in a burgundy, peach, and sage
floral, with matching pillows and sheets in a beige and sage win-
dowpane plaid.

When Sharon spent a weekend with us over the summer,
she'd recognized it instantly. "Oh. Eddie Bauer Home."

"You don't like it?"

"No, it's lovely—it looks just like the catalog. Not that there's anything wrong with that!"

Well, stagy or not, I loved the sense of safety and retreat. Getting ready for bed that night, I tried playing Massive Attack's first CD, but it felt off, and I ditched it for Chaka Khan and Rufus's *Best Hits*, because that night was a night I really needed someone to tell me something good. Listening to the album, one of my old favorites, I thought again how much something about Juno Dromgoole reminded me of pre-chunky Chaka Khan. They were certainly both big-breasted and brassy, but there was much more to the resemblance. To me, they shared an anarchic sexuality that was like the woman in one of Anaïs Nin's books who makes a man looking at her for the first time think, *Everything will burn!*

As I turned off the bathroom light and slipped into bed, I asked myself: Was feeling Stefan lost to me in his depression why I had been thinking so much about Juno? Or was it free-floating middle-age madness? If so, then why couldn't I be fantasizing about a red Miata—or learning how to snowboard? Both of those would have been much less disruptive. Or I could even have become fixated on that well-hung waiter. . . .

Lying there trying to relax, it really bothered me again that I hadn't found the right time to tell Stefan about the note on my car and the book in my mailbox—but I was so exhausted I couldn't imagine taking him through each detail. And maybe I was overreacting and it was probably no big deal, so why bother.

I fell asleep with my thoughts a hazy mix of Juno and the party. A few hours later, I woke up when Stefan crawled drunkenly into bed, saying that Didier had passed out on the living room couch.

Pathetic, I thought, but while Stefan was out right away, it took me a while: I kept fantasizing myself and Juno across the street in Didier's Jacuzzi. I did my own bed check, keeping my hands above the covers. I didn't want to wake up surprising myself.

7

WHEN the phone shrilled through my dream, I was doing something really clichéd, like rubbing an ice cube (or maybe a whole ice tray) on Juno's glossy lips. There was even background music, like one of those slow scenes in a movie that the director hopes will help sell the sound-track CD. It was Les Nubians singing *"Embrasse-moi lentement, est-ce que ma bouge te mente?"* Yow.

Struggling out of this interlude and back to consciousness, I almost batted the phone from the night table trying to get the receiver. In my confusion, I did push some David Handler and Ken Follett paperbacks off the edge but didn't bother reaching for them.

"Bad vibrations!" Polly Flockhart was screaming on the line. "I feel them—danger! Hurry!" And our New Age-y neighbor hung up, but what the hell was she talking about?

I sat up, rubbed at the sleep crumbs in the corners of my eyes, and realized that her call wasn't another one of Polly's fantasy trips; I *did* feel vibrations—as if a huge truck were parked outside our house. Was I still dreaming? If so, I wanted to get back to Juno without any interruptions.

It was just after 3 A.M. Stefan started to wake up. "What's going on?" he drowsed. "Is there a fire?"

His question made me think that I smelled smoke, faintly —but why wasn't there any smoke detector buzzing in the house? Was I really awake? And it sure felt like the bed and walls were vibrating. I snapped on my light, shook Stefan fully awake, grabbed my robe, and we rushed downstairs. That's when we heard a rumbling for real, and loud. The smell of smoke (or something) was far more intense, but, rushing around the downstairs rooms and turning on the lights, we found nothing.

We'd been so intent on searching, we hadn't bothered checking the front hall.

"Nick—look." Stefan pointed at flashing lights shining through the glass panel in the door. I tore it open. A fire truck and a Michiganapolis police car hulked down at the curb, looking as bizarrely out of place as a hippo in a rock garden. But that wasn't all we saw.

There was a smoldering stump where our wooden country-style mailbox used to be, and the unpleasant smell of burned and soggy wood was now as shockingly sharp and putrid as dog's vomit.

Stefan backed away from the door, but I surged barefoot down to the curb, with only the thin robe over my shorts. A Conan-type cop approached me and said they had just gotten there—a neighbor had called in the fire. Behind him a fireman was putting away the hose he'd used to douse what remained of our mailbox.

Suddenly Polly, in thongs and an orange-and-purple paisley terrycloth robe, was rushing down the block to us. "Nick! Nick! Are you guys okay?" Closer, she started spilling her story out: "I called the police because I felt there was *danger* on the street, and when I looked out my front door, I saw your mailbox on fire." She hugged me fiercely, and I let her, feeling grateful for the momentary comfort and for her warning phone call. I'd always been put off by her spaciness, but maybe I was wrong to mock her. I disengaged myself and thanked her several times, but she held on to my arms as if she feared I'd do something dangerous—or float away.

She told the cop where she lived and said they could question her there if they needed to, made me promise to call her for any reason at any time, and headed back up the block.

I stared at the remains of our mailbox, stunned, assuming that I was witnessing the escalation of whatever had started with the death-threat flyer on my windshield and the book left in my EAR mailbox. My question, What could be next? had been answered. And like a movie sequel, this brought back the terror of last spring when Lucille was the target of what looked like hate-crime harassment, some on campus, some at her and Didier's home just across the street.

My first thought was that someone at SUM, someone in my department, was really out to do more than just scare me. This wasn't a note or a book—this was arson, violence. But why? What had I done? What had I said? I'd never been especially popular with the other faculty, so why would someone target me now?

The cop asked if he could talk to me inside, and I said of course. I trailed back up to the house with its gaping front door, aware that lights were flashing on up and down the street and people were looking out windows and doors to find out what was happening. I felt exposed and very foolish in my shorts and robe—and chilled—but I tried to walk back inside with dignity, not "scuttle," as Juno claimed I did in Parker Hall. Juno. What would she say if this had happened to her?

As I closed the door and introduced Stefan, I watched the cop quickly check the two of us out and register that we were a couple, but I didn't pick up even a bat squeak of hostility. He introduced himself to me (again?), and for the first time to Stefan, as Officer Decker Cholodenko. Great name, I thought, eyeing his massive chest and arms. If he couldn't deck someone, who could?

I led them both to the living room and waved Cholodenko to a chair. He sat and readied his metal report case and pen. I could clearly register what he looked like now that we were inside. He was about thirty, with close-cropped blond hair, around six-foot-five, muscular and handsome in a steely, blue-eyed Clint Eastwood way, though he had to have competed professionally as a bodybuilder—he wasn't just big, he was lean. I gave him both our names again and told him how long we'd lived in the house.

Stefan sat by the fireplace, looking lifeless in his CK sleep pants, but I realized just then that Didier wasn't passed out on the couch, or anywhere in sight. "Didier went home?" I asked Stefan, who shrugged and looked around as if he'd just noticed, too. So that's why the front door had been unlocked.

Officer Cholodenko started to take notes, filling in a form, asking for us to spell our names, say how long we'd lived there. "Has this ever happened to you before?" His neutral voice was pleasantly raspy.

"No." I was answering all the questions because Stefan was too freaked out to talk.

Cholodenko pointed to Stefan. "He okay? Does he need to see a doctor?"

"I'm fine," Stefan said, his weary, distant voice belying the comment.

"Sir, are you sure?"

I'd only dealt with SUM's Campus Police Detective Valley before, and he was rude and homophobic, so Cholodenko's businesslike neutrality seemed almost like warmth in comparison.

"He'll be okay," I said.

Cholodenko nodded, his eyes unblinking. "Have you had trouble with any neighbors recently?"

"What kind of trouble?"

He gave a massive shrug. "Trash, loud music, arguments, barking dogs, whatever."

"Nothing. Not in the four-plus years we've lived here." I didn't add that aside from Lucille and Didier across the street and Polly down the block, there were only a few neighbors we knew more than just to say hello to and chat about the weather, so the question was embarrassing. Maybe we had the native

New Yorker's general suspiciousness and a need of keeping some distance, but it suddenly seemed like an outmoded and inappropriate custom.

"Wait a minute," I said. "You really think neighbors could have done this?" I chewed on that. It was always possible that a neighbor might have torched our mailbox, and that was a worse prospect in some ways than a crazed colleague—or even a disgruntled student. But I'd never picked up any hostility in the neighborhood against me or Stefan. In fact, it was the opposite.

Many of our neighbors were elderly and given to strolling. As they passed, we often got friendly compliments about the new roof we'd put on, the ugly arborvitae we'd removed and replaced with less ordinary shrubs, the in-ground sprinkler system that made sure the lawn was green and not seared-looking. People even told us we were much better neighbors than the previous owners—because we raked our leaves. "See?" Stefan had said. "Nobody cares what you are—all that counts is taking care of your property—and improving it."

"It could be kids who live around here," Cholodenko reasoned.

"But wouldn't they toilet-paper a tree or throw eggs at the house?"

"No, the cool thing is whacking mailboxes with bats, but sometimes that's not enough—"

"I'm going to bed," Stefan announced bitterly. "I can't handle this." He moved off to the stairs like a beautiful zombie.

I felt the urge to explain Stefan's behavior and describe how freaked out he was last spring when Didier's and Lucille's home was vandalized, how the unexpected invasion of violence had triggered feelings about Stefan's parents' years in concentration camps. I also felt very protective of Stefan and didn't want to share something so intimate with a stranger. Yet this was a police matter, I thought, and eventually I might have to.

Cholodenko didn't even comment on Stefan's reaction, no doubt because he'd seen lots of intense responses in his police work.

"You two were involved in a murder last year," he said to me. "On campus, right?"

I nodded. "But this can't be connected, since what happened last year was resolved. Completely resolved."

Cholodenko shook his large, handsome head as if he were a statue in a Steven Spielberg movie come to life to warn a traveler. "Either one of you, or both of you, could have been targeted because you pissed somebody off. Or because you're well known."

I challenged that: "Why now?"

Cholodenko frowned, patently at a loss to offer a reason.

"I think I may be getting harassed for something else." I told him about the death threat and the Dante paperback left in my mailbox at Parker Hall.

"Do you have the flyer?"

I explained I thought I'd thrown it out without thinking. He looked either disappointed or suspicious.

"But I have the book."

"You can't compare that to a possible death threat, or even arson, which is a felony. And you think some professor is behind all this stuff?" Cholodenko was trying not to smile. I figured he was picturing a bunch of hapless old farts with leather patches on their worn corduroy jackets. But he had no idea what a poisonous crew lurked over there at EAR.

"Let's say you're right, Dr. Hoffman. Then what's it all about?"

Helplessly, I said, "I have no idea." That's when it all came avalanching down on me. I was exhausted, upset, and mildly hung over. "Okay, I may be paranoid, I admit it."

But I was relieved when Officer Cholodenko said that he would pass the report on to the criminal investigation unit and they would get back to me. That seemed positive.

"Is this kind of vandalism common around here?"

"Not really—not arson so much. But that doesn't matter. We're going to take this very seriously, and the perpetrator could get five to ten years in jail if convicted."

Well, I found that reassuring.

Cholodenko rose. "Meanwhile, you should talk to all your neighbors, have them keep an eye out for anyone suspicious, get with your Neighborhood Watch if there is one, and speak to the postal inspectors. If your address is listed in the phone book and the SUM directory, think about having it removed. Put some lights on timers in the front rooms to discourage anything like this happening again. And you might want to consider installing an alarm system if you don't already have one," he advised on the way out. "Your exterior lighting's good, but you can never be too safe."

He handed me a pamphlet on victim's rights and his card. His speech and his massive presence had given me a strange lift, but then he was gone, and I crashed, feeling overwhelmed, threatened, besieged. We had been violated.

It was after 4 A.M. I locked up, checking the door twice, shut off the lights, and plodded upstairs as wearily as Willy Loman. I cursed whoever was after me or Stefan or both of us, trying to figure out when I could get to Builders Square the next day to get a new mailbox—preferably one that was fireproof, bomb-proof, and covered with barbed wire.

Stefan was sitting up in bed looking absolutely dazed. "This is how it starts," he said. "With fire."

I could not think of a goddamned thing to say that would de-fuse Stefan's growing dread and not make him angry, so I crawled into bed to hold him, but Stefan pushed me away. "I don't want to be touched—I feel too raw."

Of course I understood how this incident could be trigger-ing Stefan's secondhand memories of what happened to his family in the Holocaust. But I was pretty fucking offended at be-ing shut out, not allowed to comfort Stefan. It wasn't fair. And hadn't the torched mailbox happened to me, too? Why was the focus always on what Stefan felt?

"I'm not really sleepy," I said. I headed back downstairs to the security of my study, which Sharon had christened "Mal-maison"—Napoleon's favorite palace outside Paris—because of the vaguely Empire-style desk, the floor-to-ceiling bookcases, maroon drapes and rug, the overstuffed armchair and ottoman,

covered in a tapestry print of Watteau shepherdesses and shep-
herds in slate blue and maroon. "It's your palace," she'd said, with
appreciation. "Where you plan your campaigns."

Right now it was more like a retreat, and I sat at my large, or-
nate desk contemplating what had to be done in response to this
incident. No, it was an *attack*—I had to name it honestly. There
was nothing hysterical in that label.

But how the hell was it possible that I could have grown up
in New York City and never been mugged, never experienced
crime of any kind, yet here in the supposedly quiet Midwest I
hadn't just been involved in murders, I was now the victim of arson? Teaching wasn't supposed to be this hazardous. What
could be next? Kidnapping? Terrorism?

I felt queasy—should I tell people what happened? Keep it
from my parents? Was it going to show up in the *Michiganapolis
Tribune*? And was I facing another terrible round of publicity
that might increase my popularity with students but doom me
with everyone assessing my tenure application? God. I wondered if I was going to stop feeling safe in my own house
now—and what could be next.

I remembered a chilling line from *Mrs. Dalloway*: "The
world had raised its whip—where would it descend?"

Determined to dispel this gloom, even though it was getting
on to four-thirty, I called Sharon. We had always given each
other permission to phone no matter what the time.

"Nick! I was up—I was going to call you," she laughed,
sounding completely awake and alert. "But after seven. I didn't
think you'd be up before that—you never are. What's wrong?"

I quickly filled her in on all the bizarre happenings of the
last twenty-four hours, from my basement visitations and the
Flyer of Doom to the Dante smelling of smoke and the real
smoke of our mailbox. She was alternately appalled, shocked,
amused, and worried.

As a high-paid model, Sharon had traveled all over the
world. "But, *sweetie*," she said, "I tell you, I have never seen the
kind of turmoil you've been living with since you got to Michigan. Of course, I haven't been to the Sudan, or Texas, where ev-

erybody's got a concealed weapon, including the kids. . . . Hey—didn't you tell me once that Michigan has more toxic waste dumps than New Jersey? Maybe that's the trouble. Polluted water."

"It's not the whole state—it's just me."

"I feel like I'm watching some CNN guy reporting from a war zone. Sweetie, weren't you talking about getting a dog? I can really picture you sitting on the couch petting a dog. It would calm you down. It would calm *me* down."

"Sure, it would calm me down, but it wouldn't make life here any saner. Well, that's not true. It would help me cope, you're right. Stefan and I have talked about it, but we never do anything to make it happen. It just doesn't seem urgent enough."

"Well, I can see that. Staying sane, staying alive, is what you have to think about. So—have you got that student of yours, Angie, on the case? Is she out there looking for clues to all this nonsense?"

"I wish. Angie took a semester abroad—she's in England. I could really use her now." My former student Angie was a criminal justice major, and her expertise had been extraordinarily helpful in the past few years when I'd needed to contact the county medical examiner, search the web, or just understand local jurisdictional questions. "But there's more going on," I said.

"Well, what have you left out? You've got arson, harassment, lunatic and drunken professors—and that's just for starters."

"Believe me, there's more. Stefan's in a funk."

"So what else is new? He was miserable the last time I was there. The last two times I was there. Hell, the last—"

"I get the point. But this is worse, much worse." I supplied details, and as I did so, I wondered if I were being overdramatic and just plain insensitive. Stefan's career wasn't even in the toilet—it looked like roadkill that had lost all its juice a couple hundred tires ago. Why shouldn't he be depressed? And I remembered my mother once mocking the American imperative to enjoy life. "Happy, happy—who is happy?" Even the word itself sounded ridiculous in her slight accent. But of course that was the voice of Europe, of sense, of limitations.

"Whatever happened to the website he was going to do, to build his audience?" Sharon asked.

"Didn't I tell you? It cost hundreds of bucks, and he ended up scrapping it. He got all kinds of crazy people e-mailing him, criticizing his books. That they were too Jewish or gay or whatever. It was rude and stupid—just like call-in shows, only worse, because it's more anonymous. I tried to tell him that anyone who'd abuse a total stranger was really messed up and didn't know it—or an unpublished, jealous writer—or just a cyber-nudnick with too much free time—but he said he didn't need to deal with that shit on top of everything else in publishing."

"Wow."

"But I did something fun. He wanted to delete all the nasty mail and forget about it, but I e-mailed back from his address: 'Thank you for writing. Mr. Borowski is always glad to hear from his readers.' And I signed it 'Kelly B.' At least it made me feel better."

As if thinking aloud, Sharon said, "I know you've been worried about him buying more expensive clothes than usual. But really, that doesn't seem too nutty to me. Remember Charlene in *Designing Women* saying that she always felt better about world problems after she went shopping? Well, why should women be the only ones like that? You guys are wearing makeup and dying your hair and getting implants."

"I'm not doing any of that stuff—neither is Stefan."

"Men in general," she said with asperity. "Not you—of course, not you. But if you did, I'd still respect you."

"Good, someone would have to."

"Stefan's shopping may just be a personal style upgrade, or middle age."

"You're telling me people shopped a lot in the Middle Ages?"

Sharon ignored the attempted joke. "Listen, Nick, he's never been anybody's idea of a smiley-face kind of guy. In fact, he's one beer short of a Dostoyevski six-pack. Is he really that different now, or is it just more of the same?"

"Well, I think he may be drinking too much, with Didier, and he's been sharp with me." I'd always relied on Stefan's equanimity and common sense to anchor me, and the changes in him were more disturbing as I discussed them with Sharon. "The last time he was this depressed about his career was years ago, and he never said anything nasty to me then."

"Sweetie, he's older," Sharon observed. "It's wearing him out."

"But why can't life as it is be enough for him? We're happy together, we have a good life—when people aren't getting killed around us, at least—a wonderful home, the cabin up north, money. He's published books, why isn't that enough?"

"You mean, why aren't *you* enough?"

"I guess."

"Ask him."

"I have. He said it just wasn't the same. I know what he means, but it still hurts." I was about to mention Juno, but hesitated, since I'd dumped enough on her about Stefan and the newest wave of troubles for me at SUM.

Sharon started to say something, but I interrupted.

"Wait, wait—I've been babbling along about my life, but why were you going to call me at seven?"

She didn't hold back. "You know how you asked me yesterday about it being too long to wait, for the surgery? I wasn't honest with you. I know it's time. There hasn't been any real change, and it looks like I have to have the operation soon. I need to come out there again to consult with the surgeon."

Even though I had been a bit pushy on our last phone call, I had been working hard not to obsess about Sharon's illness, encouraging her each time she tried some new kind of therapy, because I'd been dreading a moment like this.

"So. Here it is at last," I said leadenly, "the distinguished thing."

"Is that some ad slogan for a new microchip?"

"No. Henry James said it, supposedly. When he had a stroke."

"Sweetie, if you're going to sling quotations at me, I would prefer a line like 'No wire hangers!' "

Neither of us laughed, and we spent some time arranging for me to pick her up at the Michiganapolis airport the next day, since she had already made her reservations before I called her. Her appointment was a week away, but she wanted to have some time with us before seeing the surgeon.

"But don't go anywhere yet," Sharon said, as I was yawning and ready to hang up. "If you're being threatened on campus and at home, if this is connected, why?"

We puzzled over what could be going on.

"My money's on that whacko Summerscale, that's who I like for this crime."

"That's who you *like*?"

"Sorry—too many episodes of *Homicide*. Summerscale—what a name—it sounds like something that would happen to your garden."

"Could be. I told you that he was pissed when I tried goofing about us being in the basement, and he did leave the reception for Camille drunk. But jeez, Sharon, it could be Iris Bell and Carter Savery trying to scare me into voting for Serena for chair. And even Juno warning me to support *her*."

"Honey, none of it makes sense," Sharon reasoned, "it's all too indirect and opaque. But you academics don't seem to have sensible methods of conflict resolution, so I guess anything is possible."

"Well, Didier was supposedly sleeping downstairs on the couch when Stefan came up to bed. What if—"

"What if?"

"Okay, picture him staggering back across the street, and he's trying to light up another cigar, and somehow he set the mailbox on fire."

"One match?" Sharon asked. "Even one cigar? No way. He'd have to do it on purpose, and he's your friend, isn't he?"

I reminded her of Didier's declining literary fortunes. "Maybe Didier was just feeling vicious and wanted to destroy something."

"If that were the case, he'd fly to New York and do a Viking raid on his publisher, he wouldn't take it out on a writer worse off than he is."

"But Stefan is published, so— No, forget it. You're right. It's too improbable."

"Some things never change. All the stuff that's happened to you out there is improbable. You're supposed to be teaching composition, and your students get murdered. You run a Wharton conference, and it's like that Poe story, you know, 'The Masque of the Red Death'—"

"It wasn't everybody that died! Just a few."

"Nick, for once I'd like to see you involved in a simple ordinary crime—like grand theft auto."

"Would I be stealing the car—or is mine the one that would get stolen?"

"Both. It's the only way to balance the cosmic books." Before I could protest, she said, "Okay, I'll see you tomorrow at the airport. You'll be the one playing chess with Death, right? And don't worry, we'll figure this all out when I get there. Meanwhile, watch your back, okay?"

I hung up, trying to stifle any fears of losing her, reassured to know that she'd be staying with us at least for a week—or longer.

8

IN the morning I woke feeling as logy and miserable as if I'd been drinking all night. My arms and legs felt both tight and overstretched, the ridge over my eyes throbbed as if someone had hammered my face with a cafeteria tray, and I could tell that my catalytic converter had broken down; my breath was toxic enough to take a few bites out of the ozone layer.

I Sasquatched my way to the bathroom, filled the sink with cold water, and dunked my head in like Hughie Lewis in his first music video, wishing I had the ice cubes, too. I didn't feel much better afterward, but as I toweled myself dry, I realized I was en route to being awake. And if worse came to worst, I only had sixteen hours left before I could go back to bed. I gargled a few times, took an unhealthy dose of Extra-Strength Tylenol, found my robe, and left Stefan snoring wetly in bed.

Each step I took down the staircase was a reluctant one, bringing me closer to the obscenity at the curb. If I were an artist in Tribeca, I suppose I could have turned the whole nightmarish experience into a performance piece, but that wasn't an option, and all I felt brave enough for was a glance at the jagged black stump while I picked up the *New York Times* from the front step. I hurried back inside as if there was a chance it could wrench itself from the ground and come stinking up the walkway at me, demanding justice and revenge.

I found it reassuringly familiar to slip the rubber band off the paper as always once I got to the kitchen. But this time when I unfolded the *Times* and opened it up to check out the headlines, a sheet of heavy white paper fell out. An advertisement?

No. When I turned it over, it read

NEXT TIME IT COULD BE YOU.

Well, I suppose that was kind enough—it wasn't an absolute threat, more like a conditional one.

I glared at the message as if I had superhero X-ray eyes and could somehow see the image of the asshole who had snuck to the house after 6 A.M.—when the paper was delivered—and put it there. It wouldn't have been the delivery boy, though I suppose the police would ask him when I called Cholodenko.

Putting up a pot of the strongest coffee we had, I said aloud, "If."

If I called Cholodenko. One look at the message, and it was Baccarat-clear that this charming missive was the product of a laser jet printer, on paper anyone could buy at Office Max or Kinko's or the SUM bookstores, just like the flyer. Nobody clever enough to be pursuing me like this would have left any fingerprints, either. So what was the point of calling the police for another visit right now? I had Sharon's arrival to think of, the guest bedroom to prepare, and a hundred other excuses for pushing this latest little assault away.

I had pissed someone off, royally. Sooner or later he—or she—would want to tell me why, or what was the good of all these hits? Let the cops work on the arson, on the worst thing that had happened so far, and maybe Sharon and I could figure out between us what was poisoning my well. Though I didn't relish the thought of either one of us questioning our neighbors to see if they'd noticed anyone sneaking around the house in the morning.

That's when I felt chilled. As the coffee perked through the

Chemex machine (slow, but better than the stuff Mr. Coffee and even Krups coffee makers produce), I thought about the time between Stefan coming to bed last night and Didier weaving home across the street—and Polly's phone call. A couple of hours in which the front door was closed but not locked. If someone was sneaking around my car, my mailbox at Parker, setting a fire in front of the house, and then monkeying with the newspaper right at the front door, what was to have stopped them from trying to break in during the night? Only it wouldn't have required any breaking, just entering if they'd simply tried the door.

Shit—shit—shit.

Like Donald Sutherland and Stockard Channing in *Six Degrees of Separation*, I started dashing through the downstairs rooms, looking for signs of damage or theft. Something we would have missed in the middle of the night when all we were looking for was smoke or flames.

I may even have scuttled, I didn't care.

There was nothing especially valuable that I was worried about, and yet everything was, every single book and framed photograph and unused souvenir ashtray was instantly as poignant and irreplaceable as if it had been rescued from calamity in a frantic car ride. Everything looked normal, though, in its place—and yet abnormal, a hostage to whoever was trying to make me crazy, and was perhaps a few Double Jeopardy questions away from succeeding if I hadn't been so tired.

I found Stefan slumped in the kitchen over a cup of the coffee, inhaling it as if it were a bowl of steaming water and he had the flu. Haggard, uncombed, and unwashed, he looked even less ready than I was to take a line-dancing class. He glanced a question at me, too groggy to even croak it out.

"Nothing," I said. "Nothing." I guess I meant nothing new had happened. Hell, I hadn't even told him about what had happened already as prologue to last night's disaster. But looking at him, I didn't have the heart to mention the flyer and the book—it would be piling too much on him.

The morning called for desperate measures, so I started fry-

ing up some Bob Evans sausage, glad my parents weren't there
to make any comments about my eating pork (we'd grown up
with the odd split of many New York Jews: kosher at home but
not "out"). Then I started making French toast just as my
mother did: from thick slices of the extra challah I always kept in
the freezer for just such an emergency. I toasted them lightly
first to get out the moisture and make them soak up more of the
egg, milk, cinnamon, and vanilla extract batter. Then I opened a
new jar of real maple syrup from the Upper Peninsula.

It settled me down to be making breakfast, and making
something my Mom did. She was so orderly when she cooked,
so calm. We ate in silence, and soon after we had cleaned up,
showered, and dressed, the phone started ringing and didn't
stop for most of the morning. First it was Polly, then it was
neighbors, and neighbors of neighbors, all calling to tell us how
shocked and sorry they were, and did we need anything?

The calls were just the beginning. We were soon besieged as
people started dropping by, many of whom we'd never met. They
appeared with flowers from their garden, Hallmark cards, baked
goods, casseroles, pies, stews—just as if bringing food to a
house of mourning. It was as miscellaneous a crowd as you'd
find following a piercing-voiced guide at a museum. Polly
Flockhart came by and all but installed herself in the front hall
as a kind of concierge, sharing commiseration and directing
people to the kitchen or living room, depending on their offering.

"I called in sick today," she told us. "I just sensed that History didn't need me as much as you did." She meant the department she worked in as a secretary, not the Muse.

I may have mocked to Stefan her perpetual tan, her many alternative universes, and her gypsies-tramps-and-thieves ward-
robe, but today I just felt grateful to see her. And she was having
a ball as our tragedy doyenne. Bravo.

At one point there could have been twenty or thirty people
drifting in and out, clucking their concern, telling us what a
lovely home we had, introducing themselves if we couldn't remember who they were, or apologizing for not having made an

effort to get to know us sooner. Most were retired, and seemed mildly pleased to have something exciting to be involved in that didn't call for signing a petition or complaining at a city council meeting.

One whippet-thin, white-haired couple in matching maroon Izod track suits and white Turntec sneakers said, "It takes something bad for people to come out of their shells, doesn't it? Floods, power failures, operations—this." They'd brought donuts from the Gnome Shoppe, one of Michiganapolis's best bakeries.

I felt heartened and overwhelmed by the outpouring of sympathy and neighborliness, and wondered if I'd need to have my cholesterol checked after indulging in all the goodies. When the calls died down, the doorbell stopped ringing, and Polly had cleaned up in the kitchen and reassured us that she was there for us, "asleep or awake," Stefan went to call Didier to see if he wanted to work out.

I put on Pergolesi's *Stabat Mater* to clear the house of the vibrations of all the people tromping through that morning, and to help me calm down and think. I poured myself some more coffee, sliced a piece of coffee cake that Polly had brought, and took myself out to the sun room.

I thought about what had happened to me, to us, so far, and sought connections. The two printed messages didn't seem the most significant aspects of the case because they weren't remotely metaphorical. Their meaning was unshaded by irony or symbolism—and they were in a sense mass-produced. So of course was the Penguin paperback of Dante's *Inferno*—but somebody had gone to the trouble of smoking it up. Was it meant to be a prelude to the actual smoke and fire? If so, it was elegant and even subtle. I played with all the associations I could come up with, as if arranging and rearranging Scrabble tiles on my stand to try scoring big points. Hell, torment, burning, fire, literature, damnation.

That led nowhere but to silliness as I started thinking of barbecues and S'mores.

Stefan appeared in the doorway. "Didier's hung over worse

than I am. He sounds like Linda Blair in *The Exorcist*. He said he'd rather go to hell than work out."

"Sometimes working out *is* hell," I said, suspicious of Didier's choice of words.

"I'm going to saw down the stump outside before I get the new mailbox."

I'd thought of doing it all myself, but since Stefan had momentarily come out of his funk, I figured it would be good for him to keep active. We talked about covering the spot with topsoil and grass seed, and about the replacement we'd put right next to where the old one had stood.

"One of those metal ones this time," he suggested. "They're easy to drive into the ground with a mallet. You don't need to dig a post hole or mix up any cement. And when I put it in, I can imagine pounding the sharp end right through the sonofabitch's heart who did this."

The syntax was twisted, but the sentiment was noble.

"Go for it."

Stefan was back soon enough, and had the replacement mailbox in the ground so quickly that aside from the slight bump next to it, you would never have noticed anything at all unusual. I was fully relaxed and awake by that point and ready to leave for the airport, even though my cogitations about the paperback and everything else were as useful as watching those TV cockfights masquerading as news "discussions."

As I pulled out of the driveway, Didier shambled over, looking as shiny and pale as a cue ball. "Who were all those people at your house before? What were you doing?"

I explained the night's excitement, and Didier was abashed.

"I slept through all that?" he asked.

"Apparently." And hadn't he even noticed Stefan working on the new mailbox? Jeez, he was really out of it. I wasn't sure I believed him about last night, but I didn't follow up on it because I had to meet Sharon at the airport, so I said I'd see him later and drove off. That was always a strange drive to the northwest part of Michiganapolis, a city that had evolved by trial and error and more error, rather than thoughtful planning. Founded in the

1830s as a trading post, it became the permanent capital only because Michigan legislators were afraid the British would in vade Detroit. They never had invaded Michiganapolis, so chalk up "the loneliest number" for civic planning.

Michiganapolis was an overgrown town that thought itself a city, characterless, spread out, bland. It had consistently demolished its past, most recently in the 1950s when its Greek revival homes had all been erased by highways; its downtown was perpetually moribund and microscopic; and there weren't even many good restaurants, although it was the state capital. To balance all that, however, it had one of the country's highest proportions of golf courses, which made us all proud.

Curious and anxious as to how Sharon would look and feel, I drove out to the airport past the boring succession of factories and small wholesalers that alternated between shabby and decayed, punctuated by Dairy Queens and fast food pits. It was a stretch of road I always felt like apologizing for when I picked someone up at the airport. But I didn't; I hadn't been living in Michiganapolis long enough to feel I could frame the remark the right way.

The airport had expanded since we'd moved to Michiganapolis, and now it was shiny, clean, and institutionally mauve and beige, whereas once it had seemed nothing more than an overgrown bus station you'd find in the cheap hookers' part of a town. But despite being able to read about Flights and Departures on video screens and eat a higher grade of muffin, you still fared better on connections if you drove down to the Detroit airport. And the city's flyers hadn't benefited from the new wave of airport design that gave you places like Pittsburgh's airport, where you could shop and stroll and linger. This was still one of those airports where passengers were shunted from one place to the next as if they were unruly grade-schoolers who had to be hushed and lined up by size.

I parked and wandered inside and through the security check, presided over by three chunky female guards who never should have been wearing pants or mauve uniforms that matched the airport. And they were chewing gum, which I thought was passé. Shouldn't it have been wads of tobacco?

Sharon's flight wasn't late, and she was the first one out, wheeling a small roll-aboard. She looked as if she was wearing a disguise or costume: large dark Jackie O. sunglasses, floppy hat, long black travel jumper over a white T-shirt, khaki multipocketed blazer, Mephisto walkers, and a chic leather knapsack shaped to curve against her body.

Hugging her, I asked, "Meryl Streep scouting a location?"

She laughed, smelling wonderful, feeling warm in my arms, if a bit thin. "I thought you'd get a kick out of this getup." Despite having lost weight, she seemed okay, but I didn't want to let her go, and I kept hugging her, silently praying for her health as deplaning passengers swirled around us.

She was the one to finally break away, to hold me at arm's length, look me up and down. "Not bad," she decided.

"For an arson victim?"

"For a crazy academic." She gestured down at her suitcase. "Can you get this? And can we stop at your office on campus? I really need to take a look at the scene of the crime."

"There haven't been any crimes there yet."

"Honey, sticking you down in the root cellar is a crime as far as I'm concerned, though I guess when the next twister comes through, you'll probably be safe."

"Wait a minute!" I said defensively as we took the escalator down. "We haven't had a twister in—"

"In?"

"Fuggedaboudit."

We did travel chat on the ride to SUM, Sharon complaining about how bad the food was even in first class. We parked behind Parker Hall, where Sharon descended with me to the hot and nasty basement in almost giggling disbelief. "It's as bad as you said," she observed when I let her in to my office. "Yikes. So where's Camille Cypriani? This basement is a dragon's lair if ever I've seen one."

"She can't be a dragon. She drinks too much, and she'd blow herself up whenever she tried breathing fire on anyone."

"Would you call her a gorgon, then?"

"Possibly. Medusa fits, too, only her hair's too neat."

On our way back to the stairs, Byron Summerscale barreled past us with an overflowing briefcase, muttering about "traitors" and "murderers." He scowled at us. Sharon turned to watch him disappear into his office.

"Did that professor just go into a supply closet? He did? Nick, this school is too crazy, you have to get out before you turn into the Mad Hatter." I reminded her that I had explained about Summerscale's office, but she seemed dubious.

As we walked out of Parker, Cash Jurevicius came tearing past us, heading for the basement. I called after him, "What did you mean about Byron Summerscale? At the party?" That stopped Cash dead, and he wheeled on us, enraged. "My grandmother *loathed* him. He's foul, he's a beast, he's evil. He doesn't deserve to live any more than Camille Cypriani does."

Sharon muttered, "Kiss your mother with that mouth?" and she yanked me away before I could reply. She hurried me to the car. "Sweetie, I thought that guy's head was going to start spinning around," she said as we drove off. "He's so cute—looks like a tennis player turned male escort—but he's so unhappy. What's the deal—is he the bastard grandson or something?"

I explained Cash's anomalous situation and reminded Sharon about what had happened to the Jurevicius Library, and how Cash might reasonably feel outraged. "But what he's got against Summerscale, I don't know."

"They're both down and out, maybe that's enough."

Stefan looked very pleased to see Sharon when we got home, and he seemed livelier than he had in days. Perhaps the simple act of repairing the night's damage made him feel less helpless, less at sea.

Sharon followed us into the kitchen, where Stefan poured lemonade and she asked him, "Did anyone get killed since Nick left for the airport?"

"That's no joke, given the way things have gone the last few years. Sometimes I wonder if I'm more than unlucky, if maybe I'm cursed."

"Cursed?" Stefan asked. "You? What for?" I almost heard

him thinking that if anyone was cursed, it had to be him.

I shrugged.

Sharon patted my hand. "No, it's this damned place. I swear it has to be. It is not your karma. This campus, this town, is like that subdivision in *Poltergeist*. Something terrible must've happened here once, and you all just happen to be the ones paying for it. But at least you're alive."

She paused and turned a little red. "I didn't mean that—"

But now the subject of her tumor had been raised, and we asked her to report on her summer again. We'd heard about the esoteric healing before, the magnets, everything, but somehow it was as if we needed to close the door on all that now.

"Nothing worked. I wanted it to. I thought something would shrink it at least, if not make it disappear, but I'm back where I started. And I still do not want to have surgery. *Brain* surgery! They're going to cut into my head. It's hard to be brave about that. What if they make a mistake and I end up like Kathie Lee Gifford?"

I wanted to reassure her, but I knew from previous talks all the risks involved, and that there was no way to be certain she'd come out of the surgery unharmed.

"You guys have to promise me not to fall apart," she said lovingly. "No matter what happens to me, you have to hold on to each other, and to yourselves." Deeply moved, Stefan hugged her, and then he headed to a presemester meeting with Peter De Jonge, a graduate student from the improbably named Michigan town of Neptune.

"Is that place for real?" Sharon asked.

"Oh, yeah, it's about an hour south of here. It's historic because of all the houses from the 1830s and a little later that were never torn down. It was in the running for state capital, but lost out, and I think just faded and died."

"Why the bizarre name?"

"Well, I think it was settled by New Englanders who wanted to remember the sea."

"I suppose Neptune's better than Cod or Mackerel."

"And better than Hell, Michigan. Or Climax."

Sharon signaled her disbelief by pouncing on the chaotic assortment of goodies the neighbors had brought by. We took some food to the sun room, where she admired the roses of Sharon that were still in bloom near the deck. We had the purple ones as well as the pale pink ones with red inside.

"Roses of Nick just wouldn't sound the same, would they?" I asked. I told her about the White Studies initiative.

"You think it'll happen?"

I shrugged. "It may not get support on campus, but parts of Michigan are very conservative—right-wing churches, the Klan, Michigan Militia. So you never know."

"Don't get into it, okay? I don't want you studying the semiotics of home fries."

I promised, and we sat back in silence a while.

Sharon smiled and breathed in. "I love being here."

"It's a great house."

"It's not the house. It's you. It's you and Stefan. I wish I had someone who loved me as much as he loves you."

"But I love you."

"Oh, sweetie, I know you do, and it's one of the things that's been keeping me sane. But— Even when Stefan's depressed, he still looks at you—. Oh, I don't know how to describe it. He enjoys you, he appreciates you, but it's more than that. There's a kind of force field around you two, between you."

I was a little embarrassed, but I enjoyed hearing Sharon's assessment. Why wouldn't I?

"Some people are together for fifteen years and you sense fatigue or resignation, but with you guys, it's more a sense of pleasure or comfort. Ease."

"That's me," I said. "I'm an emotional pair of fuzzy slippers."

Sharon ignored that. "And because you have each other, I'm sure Stefan's going to straighten up and fly right. Eventually. Maybe even being worried about what might happen to me is good for him. But if you want me to, I'll talk to Stefan by myself, and see how he's doing."

"Thanks." I leaned over and kissed her.

"You know, I think I've dealt with aging pretty well. I haven't gone berserk with plastic surgery like plenty of ex-models I could tell you about. But imagining I could be disfigured, that one whole side of my face could never move again—"

I understood. Sharon was a woman used to being admired, even in her forties, and the thought that people might stare at her because there was something wrong with her face had to be disorienting.

"It worries me, too," I said. "That you won't want to be close to me, that you'll be ashamed or something."

"Sweetie, I promise: even if come out looking like Quasimodo, I'll still want you around."

"That's because you'll need help with those church bells."

She smiled, and in this atmosphere of complete honesty, I said, "I have something terrible to confide to you, something I'm really ashamed of. I haven't even mentioned it to Stefan."

"You're having an affair? Don't look at me like that, Nick. It wouldn't shock me. You're good-looking, you're middle-aged, Stefan's been moody and distant, even though he adores you." She shrugged. "It's human nature. I would understand."

"This is worse."

"Worse? What could be worse?"

Shamefacedly, I told her all about Juno Dromgoole, about my very sudden and startling attraction to her, how I had thought it was just an enjoyment of her theatricality, but after our time in the pool and having lunch together, after the fantasies and the dreams, it was clearly more.

Sharon asked, "You're sure it's sexual? I mean, you're not just interested in trying on her clothes, are you?"

"*No.* I'm not a transvestite. I've never been. You know that."

"Easy—"

"I want to *screw* her," I wailed, astonishing myself with the ferocity of this desire not just for Juno but for a woman.

Sharon lost it, laughing and hugging herself and me. "Oh, Nick, I always thought you were pretty straight, with a nice respectable lover and steady employment, and your belief that one student at a time, you'd make America safe for literacy. But I guess you're just straighter than either one of us realized, huh?

Though I suppose there's something kind of gay about wanting to sleep with anyone who has Tina Turner hair. Unless you're exaggerating. Is Juno really that wild-looking?"

I assured her that Juno was very *caliente*.

"And you really want to have sex with her? You're sure? You fantasize about it? What kind? SWAT team sex—in and out? Or romantic, leave 'em trembling sex?"

"I can't have both?"

She pretended to consider that. Then, "So what are you hoping for? What do you expect?"

"I don't know—it's not like I'm Hart Crane finally bedding a woman after hundreds of men. I can't imagine I'm going to feel 'healed, original now, and pure' like he did."

"Only a poet would feel that about anything."

"Sharon, Sharon, what should I do?"

"Don't tell her best friend and hope she'll pass it on, whatever you do—this isn't junior high. Around your department that's the kind of thing that would get somebody murdered. Not that anything's going to happen unless Juno wants it to. Like that Lene Lovich song, remember? 'I call all the shots, baby I say when.' "

"Should I tell Stefan what's going on?"

"Not now, not ever. This isn't Jimmy Carter confessing to *Playboy* he has lust in his heart, this is really serious, and Stefan doesn't need any more uncertainty in his life right now. Neither do I, honey—please don't have *too* much of an identity crisis right now. Stefan needs you, I need you. You can't go running off to some motel with a heart-shaped vibrating bed."

"You think I don't know that? I just don't understand this: it's always the other way. A straight man discovers he's attracted to another man. That's how the story always goes. I do not want to be a trendsetter!"

"But it's not that unusual. You hear a lot about lesbians suddenly being attracted to men late in life."

"I'm not a transvestite, I'm not a lesbian."

"It was an analogy. Sorry. So you've never—?"

"Of course not. I would have told you. And I've never even

thought about it much. I notice women, of course I do, when they're pretty, or stylish, or carry themselves well."

"Thank you." She bowed her head. "Maybe it's always been more than that, since you came out so young. Maybe you just thought it wasn't sexual. But whatever, this is all a bit too exciting for me right now. I need to lie down some."

We headed upstairs with her bags. Sharon hadn't been able to get the neurosurgeon she needed at SUM's medical school to squeeze her in until the following Monday, so she wasn't in any rush. I let her unpack and settle in.

I drove back to campus, having forgotten to check my mail when I brought Sharon over, and I entered Parker a bit nervously, given everything that had been happening lately.

As if to confirm my fears, there was a note in my mailbox from Serena Fisch, asking to see me right away.

9

ENTERED Serena's new office—the inner EAR suite—with trepidation, like an errant schoolboy. While Serena—one of the lost Andrews Sisters—always had a certain harsh charm, as acting chair she had become more aloof than before. Gone was her edgy, fiery Madeline Kahn in *Frankenstein* chic—she had cooled and hardened. It was as if there were some kind of administrative spell people fell under when they assumed positions of power. Even the way they looked at others changed: *de haut en bas*. Since her elevation to acting chair, I'd felt a small sense of loss because she seemed unwilling to fraternize with lowly humans.

However, in one way Serena had stayed completely herself. She had banished the spartan look of Coral Greathouse's office. Serena had hung lavishly framed Pre-Raphaelite exhibition posters and prints on the walls, put down an oriental rug, and covered tacky chairs with colorful throws or camouflaged them with vivid pillows, giving the room a rich and somewhat disarming glow. It was clear that she meant to stay.

"Come in, come in," she said when I knocked. "You know,

Nick," she said as soon as I sat down, "I'll need to appoint someone new to your tenure review committee, since I can no longer serve on it."

Her tone and the stiff, watchful way she held herself made me want to say, "Godfatha, out of the respect that I show to you and your family—" but I stifled the rogue impulse.

Serena prompted me with, "Any suggestions?"

I couldn't believe she would consider my choice, or that this was even an appropriate conversation, but all I could think of saying was the truth: that I was dim enough not to have realized before that moment that a change needed to be made. Serena's news was a blow, because I had counted on her support and seniority on the committee, and there weren't that many people who liked me in EAR. My former officemate Lucille Mochtar did, but she was away for the semester. Still, if Serena was chair when my application moved out of the committee, that would be good, I thought, however unsure I was about her being the right person for the job.

"Can I get back to you?"

"Whatever you say," she replied with unbelievable graciousness. "I'm amenable to waiting to hear from you."

I realized this smoothness must be connected to the inevitable election for permanent chair, even though Juno hadn't publicly announced she would run. Serena wanted me on her side, no matter how it all played out.

"So, what did you think about yesterday's unveiling?" she asked, and it took me a moment to realize she was referring to the president's idea for a new program, though I couldn't tell whether she was for or against. I played it safe.

"The task force is bound to be controversial."

"All new ideas are," Serena said calmly. Did she support it or not? I wasn't sure, and I felt like I was dangling from a ledge there. Serena didn't give anything away about her stand, but simply concluded with a cheerful, "We'll just have to see what happens." She was as blithe as some contemptuous eighteenth-century French countess tossing coins out of her carriage to peasants, the kind of woman they would have torn from her coach and ripped to shreds if given a chance.

"You know, Nick, I wish there were a better solution to your housing problem than putting you in the basement. Is there anything you need to be more comfortable?"

I was not used to being treated so well by an administrator, and I was tongue-tied—but not for long.

"An air conditioner would be great," I blurted.

"Why not?" Serena made a note on a Post-it pad and nodded.

Outside in the hall I was met by Iris and Carter, who pounced as if they'd been waiting for me. "It's monstrous—disgusting," they said, ranting about White Studies and how they had to fight it before it turned the college and EAR into a joke.

That was a rearguard action, I thought, if ever there was one. Iris and Carter wore the greedy, pinched faces of mean little kids spreading misinformation about sex. They obviously wanted to whip me into a similar frenzy, but if the Whiteness Studies idea took off, as stupid as some people thought it may be—and the department supported it fully—then my opposition could be a problem.

"I've got a headache," I said unimaginatively, and fled to the basement, suddenly smiling when I remembered the advice in *Scream*: "Don't run upstairs."

In my office to briefly do some paperwork, I half expected to be waylaid by Byron Summerscale or Cash Jurevicius. But it was Juno who arrived at my door in a cloud of perfume, which suited her as well as Jove's shower of gold did him. She had her hair back in a fat ponytail under a black velvet baseball cap with velvet leopard print edging the bill, and wore a black jumpsuit with a leopard-print scarf around her neck and a pirate's chest's worth of gold bracelets on each arm.

"Holy shit," she said, checking out my office. "This is truly, really and truly, a fucking Black Hole of Calcutta. And I mean that sincerely. But it's not as dismal as what passes for a brain in President Littleturd. Could you believe him last night?" She settled into the comfortable chair I had for students, making herself so much at home I expected her to ask for a drink.

"You think White Studies is a bad idea?"

Juno erupted. "Hel-lo? It's not even a fucking idea! It's a trend, it's a twitch, it's toe jam! 'Customer demand'? What students would want to study being white unless they were racists or Nazis? Why don't they just sell the whole fucking school to the skinheads, if that's what they're after? Most students can't even write a decent essay, and now they're going to be studying the semiotics of mayonnaise?!"

I didn't want to reveal what I thought, and hated having to temporize. "Well, some respectable academics find merit in the idea of *Whiteness* Studies."

"Spare me! There's no such thing as a respectable academic. They're all conspirators, maniacs, or whores."

"Which are you?"

Juno roared with laughter, as she always did when I twitted her. "A bit of all three, I suppose." Then she shuddered. "All night at that ghastly Stephen King reception I kept picturing our loathsome dean in the nude. He's so hideously fat I'm sure he's got one of those penises that just looks like a tiny mushroom bobbing on a sea of flesh. How could he and Nina possibly have sex? How would he even know if he had a woody?"

The image disgusted me, and I must have made a face, because Juno said, "Surely I'm not shocking you? Is that possible?"

"Why do you say that?"

"Well, what could shock someone like you—haven't you done it all?"

"I don't think so."

"You're joking, aren't you? No golden showers? No fisting? No bondage? No S&M? Group sex? Barebacking? Well, surely you at least have some piercings I didn't get to see in the pool." She gestured to the area of my crotch. I tried hard not to cross my legs. When I shook my head, Juno asked dismally, "I suppose you don't even have a single tattoo? No? Darling, please tell me what the good of being queer is, if you and Stefan are going to be as boring as butter and mate for life like some squalid little pair of doves?"

"Why do people assume that just because I live with a man, I'm—"

"—*interesting*? It does tend to go with the territory," Juno observed tartly. "In most cases, that is. Oh, I'm sorry," she said. "I've offended you, haven't I? Can you forgive me?"

I nodded.

"Shall we make plans to swim at the Club later this week? I really do think I can help you with your stroke. You need to reach more with your left arm. I was studying you." She seemed eager for me to say yes, but embarrassed by her attention, I just said that I would call, and Juno left.

I sat there listening to her heels fade down the hallway, drowning in her perfume and politics. If Juno was adamantly against White Studies, did that mean Serena would automatically take the other side? She'd have to anyway, as an administrator, since the idea must have approval from the provost, who oversaw all expenditures, and the dean, given that the new department or program would probably be housed in Arts and Letters.

I pondered this. The dean and Coral Greathouse were rivals, so what if something more byzantine was going on? What if Bullerschmidt was actually opposed to Littleterry's plan, but was keeping mum in the hope that when the controversy erupted on campus—as it surely would—and the idea was crushed, Coral Greathouse would be publicly dished and might even have to resign? Everyone knew that Littleterry was just chosen as a feel-good figurehead, and that the dim-witted ex-coach was generally ruled by whoever was SUM's provost. Still, could Coral Greathouse really be the power behind *this* throne?

And what was up with Juno wanting to help me with my stroke? Which stroke did she have in mind? Had I been imagining her flirtatiousness?

Just as I was about to wrap up and leave, Sharon walked in with an enormous pot of silk hydrangeas, which she set down on my desk as happily as a cat bringing its master a bird. "This place needs more life," she announced. "But there's not enough sunlight, so a real plant wouldn't survive an afternoon—" I sat there beaming while Sharon explained that on our drive from the airport, she remembered passing a store near campus that sold silk floral arrangements. She called it when she got up from her brief nap, and then took a cab over.

I hugged her, and we spent way too much time figuring out where to place the pot for maximum effect. "All this redecorating," she said when it was back on my desk. "Aren't you hungry?"

"Absatootly." I took her to Les Deux, a new bistro-type restaurant in town run by twin brothers who had graduated from SUM's nationally known School of Hotel and Restaurant Management and subsequently also studied cooking in Paris. It had recently become Stefan's and my favorite place for lunch and dinner, and the owners had joked about putting a plaque up on "our" booth.

I could only tell the slim and vivacious brothers apart because Scott, the chef, wore a blue denim chef's jacket, while Eric, the manager, didn't. Eric greeted us effusively as always, I introduced Sharon, and we were soon feasting on *moules* and *frites* and a bottle of muscadet Sharon insisted on ordering. Though located in one of Michiganapolis's ubiquitous strip malls, Les Deux was a warm, dark place with the feel of Quebec City, if not actually of Paris.

"This is lovely, so much better than the other strip malls with fast food. I know the country's turning into one big strip mall, but you do seem to have more than your fair share. And two Mongolian Barbecues? It's bizarre. I don't understand the concept. Genghis Khan, rape, pillaging, that's what Mongolians are known for. Not their cuisine. When's the last time you bought a book of *Best Dishes of the Golden Horde?*"

She seemed a bit manic, but I didn't ask her if she should be drinking or not, and she suddenly shifted gears. "This has been really hard on my folks, Nick. They said it was crazy to try any alternatives, that I should have had the surgery the same month I got diagnosed. But it's a slow-growing tumor," she said. "I did have time. I did not have to rush."

"What happened to Dominic?" He was the young pianist she'd been dating earlier in the summer.

"He wimped out. Couldn't take the stress of my being ill.

No, *thinking* about my being ill. Because I look pretty good for someone with a tumor, don't I? He started cheating on me with a soprano. And the worst kind! Driven, hard, gorgeous, young, and she works out at the same gym I do. Can you believe it? If I'd known, I would have bitch-slapped her in aerobics class. But that's what I get for dating an accompanist. God, I wish Dominic had been a singer instead. I'd take a singer any day. I could handle the temper, the depression, the jealousy and gossip, the sadistic voice coach, the vocal nodules. But an accompanist— You not only live with *his* emotional tempests, but everybody's he plays for. It's geometric group therapy, and after a lifetime in New York, if I ever hear the word *therapy* again, I will scream."

"What's wrong with therapy?"

"It's the therapy junkies that bother me. They're always talking about making progress, and finding themselves slowly, and getting in touch with their anger or their inner child, and getting better. Nobody seems to ever get well or just *stop*, no matter whether they're doing psychoanalysis, Jungian, primal scream, Gestalt, TA, Skinnerian, or Reality Therapy. You should see their faces when they talk about it: they're either bragging about how they can stand all the ugliness, how tough they are, or they look wasted, like they just got out of solitary confinement. And the jargon! Do you know what it's like at a party to have some stranger turn to you and say, 'My husband and I have boundary issues'?"

"I would just tell them 'Well, so does Bosnia-Herzegovina. You're not alone.' "

I got her laughing with that, but just as suddenly shushed her. Across the room, Juno Dromgoole was being seated with Dean Bullerschmidt and Camille Cypriani. Juno waved fondly at me (or was I imagining her warmth?). I alerted Sharon as to who they were, and she surveyed the trio. Even though I realized I was acting like a nervous adolescent, I pressed Sharon: "What do you think?"

"Honestly? Juno reminds me of that actress in *The Man Who Came to Dinner*—you know, the one somebody makes fun of: 'They say she set her mother on fire, but I don't believe it.'"

"Is that all?"

Sharon leaned across the table, keeping her voice low. "Sweetie, if you do want to sleep with a woman, you might want to work your way *up* to Juno. She looks a bit formidable for a beginner."

I tried not to laugh in case Juno, Cypriani, or the dean decided I might be laughing at them. Sharon knew something of the controversy over Camille and the coming rivalry for chair, so she followed me when I said, "Juno must be lunching with the dean to seek his support for chair, since Bullerschmidt has the power to veto any action the department takes if he wants to. Unless the dean is after Juno's help to push—or undermine—White Studies, and they're making some kind of deal. But it's so strange to see them together, given that Juno professes to loathe the man. And where does Camille fit in?"

We both glanced their way, trying to be cool. Juno was chatting away, and Bullerschmidt was apparently responding, while Cypriani looked embalmed, with what Yeats called "a gaze blank and pitiless as the sun."

Sharon sipped some more wine, telling me how amazed she was at all the latest academic hugger-mugger I'd explained to her. "And here I thought models and photographers were nuts. But they're just into sex and drugs and clothes and cars. Does any of this really matter?" she asked.

"It does to me. Michiganapolis and SUM are my home now, and I have to work here."

"Have to? Or want to? You need to get away. Oh, honey, when I was in Venice last month, I wished you were there, both of you. Not to keep me company, but to get away. To sit in one of those little squares with a well, take a gondola ride, spend just forty or fifty bucks on a wonderful dinner with a local wine. I pictured you there, loving it, loving being away."

"We could go to Venice, but that's only a vacation."

"It would be a start," she said hopefully.

"Venice gives me the creeps."

"Venice does? But what about Edith Wharton, and Henry

James, and all your other favorite writers? Everybody went to Venice."

"Rupert Everott got killed there."

"Say what?"

"In that movie with Christopher Walken. Remember?"

She nodded, and took my hand. "Nick, *The Kindness of Strangers* was a movie."

"Maybe so, but it left an impression."

"Okay, then I won't even start on Nice."

We finished lunch and signaled for the check, while I laid out to her "White Studies"—as it was probably going to be called now that the president had got it wrong—and the chaos certain to erupt on campus as the news got out about SUM's "bold new initiative."

Sharon was hopeful. "At least you're not in the middle of it, right?"

"Maybe not exactly, but didn't somebody once say that when elephants fight, the entire village gets trampled?"

"For sure," she grinned. "Hannibal did. And speaking of elephants—" We dished the dean for a while, and I recounted my previous run-ins with Bullerschmidt, most recently at the pool. But Sharon interrupted me. "If your department's going to be split over White Studies as well as the race for chair, then where does Camille Cypriani stand? Because isn't she the most powerful woman in the department now?"

We headed for my car to drive home. "I don't know what she thinks about it—it's not like we've ever talked to each other." I opened up the doors, and we got in.

"Why does Stefan hate her so much? I understand the jealousy part, but it feels like it's bigger than that."

"It is, but you can't ever tell him that I told you."

Sharon promised.

"Okay. Stefan once wanted a blurb from Camille for one of his books, but instead of letting his editor request it, he wrote her himself. It was stupid, I guess, but thinking about blurbs makes writers desperate—everyone hopes that one big endorsement by a well-known author is going to make a difference. It never does. So, anyway, Stefan wrote her a letter. No reply. Then another one."

"And probably a third?"

"Yes. Shit!" We were stopped at a light that had just changed to green, but several student bicyclists had whizzed across in front of us. "They're so careless, it infuriates me. I hate this place when the students come back."

"It was quieter in the summer," Sharon admitted. "So what about the last letter?"

"This one was even more abject than the previous two. And then she replied. She sent him back a little handwritten note on scented stationery that Stefan never forgot."

Sharon gulped. "What did it say?"

I could quote it easily, since I had not forgotten the blow either: " 'My Dear: I understood that you were making a request, not a demand. Yours most sincerely, Camille Cypriani.' Stefan was devastated, and now here she is in his very own department, lording it over him and everyone else. It gets worse. Stefan heard independently from a writer friend much later that Cypriani never writes her own blurbs—she lets editors or publicists or writers themselves do it. She doesn't care who, as long as she doesn't have to be involved."

A bit naively, Sharon asked me why Stefan persisted even after not getting a reply the first time, and I explained again that lots of authors feel blurbs will magically make their books successful. "But nowadays, only Oprah has that kind of power."

Driving up to our house, I was feeling companionable and relaxed until I spotted the new mailbox. It not only reminded me of the night before, but made me feel vulnerable and even a little ashamed.

Sharon instantly picked up on my distress and asked what was wrong as we pulled into the driveway, her hand on my arm.

"Shit. Replacing a mailbox that's been hit by a car is annoying, but it's no biggie. What we had to do leaves me feeling like there's a giant sign on our lawn that says VICTIM."

Inside, however, Stefan was feeling upbeat because he had a good first class, and we were sitting around talking about what we should make for dinner when the phone rang. I got it: it was Dulcie Halligan from EAR announcing that Camille Cypriani's first literary luncheon, scheduled for that coming Sunday, had been canceled because she had to fly to London for some undisclosed reason. Instead, she was inviting the luncheon guests over to her home for drinks the next evening at seven. "Flyers about the change will be in the appropriate faculty mailboxes," Halligan said primly. "But we secretaries are calling everyone on the guest list to make sure the word gets out." That was my cue to thank her for being so responsible, which I did.

Stefan blew up when I passed him the news. "What is this, a command performance? Why doesn't she just pick another Sunday? How can she ask people out just two nights after her reception? Most of us have to work—we have classes to teach, we're not paid to sit on our butts like she is."

"Easy, easy," I said. "Of course she's changing the date. She's furious that Littleterry eclipsed her last night with his idiotic announcement. Now we get back-to-back celebrations of *her*. It's a Camille-a-thon!"

"You don't have to go, do you?" Sharon asked, and we both gave her baleful looks that made her flinch. "Ouch. So it *is* a command performance, then."

Stefan railed some more, but Sharon stopped him by quietly asking if this was connected to Camille or about the mailbox being torched.

"Both," he insisted, then amended it. "The mailbox. Of course."

Suddenly I felt afraid, too, as if I knew what Stefan was going to say.

"I was paralyzed last night, staring down at the curb, even my thoughts felt frozen, like being in a nightmare when there's something going to hurt you, something you can't see and you can't escape." He raked us with his ravaged eyes. "What if they never find out who did this to us? They probably won't. Or what if it escalates somehow? I used to feel safe here," he said.

Sharon asked, "Even with the murders over the past few years?"

Chin up, Stefan said, "Yes, actually. But now I feel trapped. It's probably Camille Cypriani who's behind it. I bet she's a pyromaniac and she's planning to burn her way through the EAR faculty."

I was amazed at this sullen outburst, amazed. "That is really crazy, Stefan. You sound just like me—that's something I would think up."

Stefan looked at me and started to chuckle. "You're right." One less turn of the screw.

"Camille isn't a criminal. You just hope she gets caught doing something, anything, so they can throw her in prison and drum her out of EAR, but that would only make her an even bigger star."

Sharon asked us more about the endowed chair, and Stefan explained that it was created by an anonymous donation. "Apparently Camille's checks don't even come through the department like those of the other faculty."

"Isn't that special?" Sharon said in imitation of the Church Lady.

"It was all presented by the provost over the summer as a fait accompli."

I added, "We've learned that's the usual time of year for doing anything sneaky or controversial, which is why I'm surprised White Studies didn't get introduced as an idea then."

"Nick—I forgot to tell you," Stefan said excitedly. "Apparently news about White Studies leaked out, and there are rumors that black faculty and students are calling for a boycott of classes next week."

I shook my head. "SUM doesn't care about mundane stuff like that, unless it goes on long enough to create bad publicity. If people want to really hit 'em hard, they should get the black players on the football team to go on strike. Even one game—wow!"

Stefan smiled and said to Sharon, "That would never happen. The joke is that SUM is a football program with a university attached. And not a very good one, either."

"University or football program?"

"Both," we said together.

"I want to know more about Camille. Does she get scented envelopes?" Sharon wondered. "Is she too important for regular paychecks? Has anyone actually seen Camille's endowed chair?" Sharon asked with a pretty good Locust Valley lockjaw accent. "I mean, where is it? And what does it look like? Is it a bergère? A bar stool? A chaise longue? A recliner?"

Under this barrage of seating-related raillery, Stefan let go some more, and we set about planning dinner. Sharon sat next to Stefan and pored over a cookbook. While they did that, I kept looking at Sharon, imagining life without her. She was second only to Stefan for me, a constant source of support and insight and fun. "I'm not ready for anything to happen to her," I thought, wondering how the clouds had seemed to move into my life in just forty-eight hours. It was too eerie.

They ended up choosing something simple, and we ate in the kitchen. Over a chicken stir-fry dinner with a bottle of Meursault, I said that I'd been trying to figure out who might be holding a grudge against me (or me and Stefan) or just plain disliked me, but that wasn't getting me anywhere. "Even the fact that I'm feeling so paranoid bothers me."

"You're not paranoid," Stefan said. "Somebody burned down our mailbox."

This seemed like the time to tell him about the two notes and the Dante paperback, so I did, unsensationally, unemotionally. But even stripped of drama, the details were very disturbing.

Stefan got very quiet, set down his knife and fork, breathed deeply. Was he going to yell? He looked very sad when he said, "I wish you'd told me right away."

"How could I, when you've been playing the Dying Swan?"

I've read in books all the time where somebody's eyes "flashed," but had never seen it until then. I could tell he was about to say something devastating, but Sharon stopped him, stopped us.

"At least you're both healthy," she said, and we felt suitably chastened. "I'm sorry, sweetie. I didn't mean that as criticism.

But since I got diagnosed, I keep thinking about how I used to sail through a day without ever thinking anything could slow me down. And now, it's almost as if I'm cut off from people who haven't known illness or suffering. It's not that I'm in pain, really, not yet. But I am facing the possibility of an incomplete recovery from the operation—and it could be terrible. So forgive me, sometimes I come out with comments that sound a lot more bitter than I feel."

"Us, too?" I asked. "You feel cut off from us?"

"Sometimes. Not completely. And not with what happened to Stefan's parents in the Holocaust, and all your sleuthing, not when I think about all that, no."

It wasn't a very clear or satisfactory answer, I thought, but it would have to do. It might be the best she could offer right then.

I suggested lemon sherbert for dessert, but Sharon asked if we had any vodka.

"Of course, in the freezer. Why?"

"When I was in Venice at a wonderful tiny wine bar, Antico Dollo, they served a vodka and lemon sherbert *digestivo* after the meal. It was amazing."

Stefan found the champagne flutes she asked for, and as I watched her prepare our treat, I felt glad that she had gone to Europe in the summer to visit some of her favorite places—Venice, Villefranche, the Ile de Ré. After her surgery, she might not be able to fly again for a long time—and worse, she might not want to.

10

HART Crane wrote that "the bottom of the sea is cruel." Well, if he'd ever taught, he might have said the same thing about the first week of fall semester. Stunned by their loss of summer freedom and dazed by the charnel house of registration, students were confused, often chasing the right professor for the wrong course. But I felt an unaccustomed calm.

I'd arranged my fall schedule to have my three office hours all on Thursday afternoon, and even though it was the chaotic first week of classes, I enjoyed a rich, fulfilling day. While it was still too early for my writing students to have serious questions about their work, since they hadn't turned in any assignments, there was already a line to see me, and a party atmosphere out in the hallway. For someone who'd been marginalized in EAR, threatened and ignored, the two dozen students were gratifying. Too bad they couldn't see this upstairs; maybe I should set up a live feed.

And finding them there reminded me of why I'd gone into teaching in the first place, and erased the stain of craziness that had spilled like red wine across the white tablecloth of my rather ordinary life.

The students were chatting amiably, standing, sprawling, reading *Spin* and *Details*, leafing through the enormous and multisectioned first-day SUM student newspaper, sharing Arby's and Taco Bell, munching chips, popcorn, candy bars. Food was ubiquitous on campus, and students grazed all the time now; I didn't bother trying to keep my classroom a food-free zone the way other professors did. The only thing I told my students was: no fondue pots.

Most of the guys waiting in the hall wore baggy, oversize jeans with frayed bottoms, neutral T-shirts, fat beads, and side-burns. With their heads shaved or hair only a quarter-inch long all around, they looked like members of some funky new order of monks. And if you saw a bare arm, there was the tattoo of barbed wire, chains, flames, or wreaths around the biceps —these had become as common as goatees were a few years before. Only they'd be a lot harder to get rid of when boredom set in.

A small subset of the guys looked like Gap ads in sandals, cargo pants, sweatshirts, fleece vests, sling packs, and the ubiquitous blond-tipped hair. Stefan and I were still bemused by the wave of tattooing that had hula-hooped the United States in the last decade. We still remembered it as fairly déclassé when we were kids—unless the wearer was a marine. But now there were stores like *Tattoos R Us* at the mall, with its own "drive-thru," gift certificates, and coupons in the weekend supplements. An even smaller group of guys wore Bob Marley T-shirts with their dreadlocks, all wholesome and blond despite the get-up.

The women were in what I thought of as nouveau-Madonna-meets-Siouxsie-and-the Banshees: multiple nose rings and piercings under or over their lips; huge clunky shoes with solid cork heels and soles; black miniskirts or dresses under see-through black blouses; spiky hair the color of black shoe polish; and bruised-corpse makeup. There were some retro-preppies thrown in for color, their pinks and yellows as startling as tulips in a coal bin.

Yet underneath all the costuming, the borrowed attitudes, these guys and girls were still only teenagers: enthusiastic, nervous, pimply, moderately spazzed out by the start of the semester. I know they annoyed some faculty because of their general cluelessness, but they made me feel avuncular—at least at this early point. There was still time to be pissed off by the multiple-excuse students who always had a dire reason for not getting work in on time, and the students who didn't show up but expected a B, and the ones who worked hard and were hopeless but also expected a B.

As I headed into my office that afternoon after two good classes back to back in the morning, everyone smiled and waved or called out my name, and it was a bit of a rush to feel that popular. Inside, I realized that all my publicity as a crime magnet and ersatz crime solver had actually made it even easier to connect with my students. Their morbid curiosity made them more open to working on their writing with me and considering serious issues it brought up. I was a role model, or something hideous like that. I may have been old, but I was cool. Or: cool enough. Maybe I could have that phrase translated into Latin to put on my family coat of arms.

The sole break in the festive mood as I chatted with one eager student after another was the occasional slamming of Summerscale's door as he surged in and out of his closet of an office. These departures and returns always silenced whomever I was talking with and all the waiting students outside, who correctly sensed that Summerscale was not a man to laugh at. But I thought his jack-in-the-box routine was like a bad sketch on an old-time TV variety hour.

Juno bopped in at one point, catching me between students. She seemed as distracted and harassed as everyone else tended to be during the first frantic days of the semester, having to fight the traffic in town and on campus, and push through the often confused but ebullient hordes of students. SUM had 45,000 of them. That's a lot of guests or customers or content recipients or whatever they were supposed to be called in the latest administrative Humpty-Dumpty decree. I couldn't always remember.

Juno's manner changed as soon as she spoke up. "I'd like to invite you to tea some time," she said with real warmth. She was wrapped in a long leopard-print skirt that teased the top of her calves, black leather boots, and black blouse, with a leopard-print chiffon scarf knotted through her hair. She looked ready to party, not to teach, and she smelled good.

"And will you?" I asked, leaning back to take her in better.

She grinned. "Clever boy. Yes, let's check our schedules and put our heads together." She wheeled about and left me feeling mildly excited and wildly guilty. I was arranging to see Juno for, well, for what, exactly? Just tea? Would she be the crumpet? Or would I?

It wasn't until I drove home late that afternoon that I realized that nothing bad had happened all day; no one had broken my windshield or spiked my tires, left a dead squirrel in my mailbox, or otherwise threatened me. Was it over? Or was I being softened up for something worse?

Even though she hadn't been invited, Sharon insisted on coming to see "the show," as she put it, so that Thursday evening the three of us set off for Camille Cypriani's literary gathering, not knowing what to expect. Sharon had donned another kind of costume: a black, long-skirted Dolce and Gabana suit with silver slingbacks.

"You look like *Breakfast at Tiffany's*," Stefan said admiringly.

"Except Sharon has boobs and smaller feet," I pointed out, and Sharon ruffled my hair, murmuring, "Thanks." I asked, "It's a great outfit, but why did you bring that?"

"Doesn't matter where you go, you should always have something faboo to wear."

Stefan was pretty faboo himself, wearing silver silk Gaultier slacks and blazer with a sleeveless black shirt. Me, I looked okay, but I wasn't remotely in their league.

Before we left, I'd had some time to talk to Sharon about Stefan's clothes spending, and this time she warned me that if I raised it, I might start an argument. And she went even further. Since it wasn't coming from an account we shared, it really wasn't my business to bring it up. "He's not an alcoholic, Nick, and he doesn't need an intervention."

As if something not being my business had ever stopped me before. "But what's it all about?" I had pressed.

"Let him figure it out himself. He's pretty aware, most of the time, right? And he's a novelist. Maybe he's playing a part, living some fantasy. Who knows? Why not just enjoy how hot he looks? He's not beating on you, creating public disturbances, getting into fights or car accidents, sleeping around."

"True."

"Besides, you should be grateful—that is a man who wears clothes very, very well."

I couldn't disagree with Sharon's verdict.

"And that cologne, yum. Coriolan is perfect on him."

Perfect, and expensive, even when we bought it (or he bought it) at the duty-free shop coming back from Canada.

But I decided that from now on when I saw him come home with a Nordstrom's shopping bag, I wouldn't think of the credit card receipt, but picture how terrific he'd look, how many people would turn when he entered a room.

Camille Cypriani had taken up residence in a condo in a naked new Michiganapolis development well north of campus, where the houses perched on bare little rises like fat prairie gophers surveying the landscape, and the shrubs were nonexistent or stunted. Cars lined the street outside Cypriani's new home. Rumor had it that it was included with the endowed chair. If that was true, then I wondered why anyone in EAR would be burning my mailbox down instead of hers. A minimal teaching load, $175,000 a year, and a great place to live? It was enough to spark an academic civil war, let alone arson.

When we arrived, there were already a few dozen people inside, including graduate students, looking adrift in all the soulless luxury. The large, spacious condo had that strange blend of authoritarianism and chic that always results from being over-decorated. Sharon calls it Mussolini Moderne. Here the palette was silver and sage, and it helped create the feel of a stage set with impersonally grouped objects, all in threes: Venetian masks, copper vases, nutcrackers, antique glass bottles, clocks, picture frames—even bonsai trees.

There was a huge drinks table and very little to eat to soak it up. I had no idea who had been invited and who hadn't, but there didn't seem to be as many faculty members there as I'd expected, and more teaching assistants. Perhaps the faculty had had enough Cypriani worship for one week.

Bizarrely, at least to me, there was a small white baby grand in the bay window and a suited pianist playing movie themes; as we arrived he finished the theme from *Dr. Zhivago* and headed into *The Summer of '42*. The graduate students seemed to be sloshed already, with everyone else there well on the way, and a general sense of confusion reigned. What exactly were we all doing there—wasn't it a bit late in the day for a luncheon, literary or otherwise? Were people supposed to talk about books or what? At the moment, despite the confusion, it was probably going to be another typical EAR event, equal parts gossip, resentment, and quiet misery—though, of course, the surroundings were far more elegant than usual, as had been the case at Dean Bullerschmidt's house on Monday night.

The Queen Bee herself was nowhere in sight. Cash Jurevicius, however, was on hand. Despite being an adjunct, he was always invited to EAR and College of Arts and Letters functions in deference to his late grandmother. He nodded at us, not even momentarily shedding his perpetual glare of dissatisfaction. I asked Stefan why Cash bothered coming to these functions when they must make him feel cheated, excluded, and humiliated.

"Maybe that's why," Stefan observed quietly. "Didn't you tell me you heard somewhere that hatred has to be fed like a fire, or it burns itself out?"

"That's grim," Sharon said. "Where's it from?"

"*Ally McBeal.*"

Sharon made as if to smack my arm, and I ducked out of reach. We snagged glasses of tonic water and lime to start with and stood back to survey the cold, imposing room. Sharon asked me what else I knew about Cash.

"Why? Do you think he's cute?"

"Sure. And someone angry like that can go all night, even at his age. He's got so much to prove."

Stefan frowned and said he wasn't sure he wanted to know that about Cash or anyone.

I didn't have much to tell Sharon about Cash. I did say, though, that it was wildly ironic that people like Cash were called "gypsy scholars," since their lives weren't anything like the images the term conjured up. "Forget about tarantellas, colorful caravans, and tambourines. They should call them 'mine workers' to capture the sense of oppression. And since they get an intellectual version of black lung disease."

Sharon and Stefan both said, "Yuck."

Cash must have sensed we were discussing him, because he walked over, and I took the opportunity to ask him what was wrong with Summerscale, since I'd never really heard anything. I was fishing, of course, since the Malatestas had gossiped about him, but I wanted to know why Cash was so angry at the man.

Grim-faced, Cash said, "He always meets his students in bars in town, rather than his office."

"Have you seen his new office?" I asked.

Cash said he had, but this behavior predated the recent move to Parker. "And he can be very inappropriate in class. Once after he confused a student by asking him several times if he was sure he had the right answer and the student changed his mind, Summerscale yelled at him, 'Don't ever do that again! You might as well just hand me the Vaseline and bend over, because once you do that, your ass is mine, all mine.' "

"You know this for a fact?"

Cash nodded. "If Summerscale was trying to teach a lesson in not being intimidated, that was a lousy, sick way to go about it. This kind of behavior goes way back, but it's always been hushed up."

The three of us were appalled, but I asked why, if Summerscale was so blatant, he hadn't been called on this outrageousness before. Cash sneered, "Someone probably owes him a favor, or someone's taking care of him."

"By dumping him in Parker's basement?" I asked. "In a supply closet? I'm glad I don't have that kind of patronage—I'd be outdoors in a tent by now."

Stefan asked, "You're sure about the story?"

Cash nodded fiercely. "I heard it from the honors student it happened to. A decent, quiet guy. He'd never make it up."

"And he didn't complain to anyone at the Honors College?"

Sharon answered that one for Stefan. "Of course he didn't, because he was ashamed. His professor publicly humiliated him, in class—why would he make it worse by talking about it?"

"Exactly," Cash said, eyeing Sharon as if he'd suddenly noticed her, and I realized I hadn't introduced them, so I did that. They made small-to-medium talk, and I heard Cash ask her how long she was going to be in town. Was he just being polite, or hitting on her? Stefan and I exchanged a glance at the thought of them dating.

Serena Fisch arrived just then, holding herself as quietly as if her every breath gave the departmental imprimatur to this event. Stefan asked me if he could christen Cypriani with a bottle of champagne to start the semester right.

"Cool your jets. She's a battle-ax, not a battleship. But where is she?"

Cypriani emerged just then from a hallway to preside over our grim festivities in a ludicrously formal black taffeta skirt and crimson cashmere twin set with a mink collar. Her entrance was so intimidating that people hung back as if she were some nauseating, bone-thumping ride at an amusement park. She surged right over to us, issuing a regal welcome, not even concerned about or interested in who Sharon was or why she was there, though Sharon turned to her with polite interest. Was it rudeness in Cypriani, booze, or bad peripheral vision?

As Cypriani swept off, very much the grande dame, and Cash followed, Sharon confidently tagged Camille's outfit, "Oscar de la Renta."

I said, "This reminds me of Bette Davis in the party scene in *All About Eve.* But then everything reminds me of *All About Eve* these days. With a touch of *Jaws.*"

Sharon added, "I wish I'd had my Chanel couture to wear—that would have shown her," before she headed to the bathroom and Stefan sloped off for a real drink. That's when Juno—who must have been in the kitchen until then—sidled up to me in a black sheath and sheer leopard-print jacket, looking better than anything on the buffet table.

"Seeing you and Stefan together," she murmured, "always gives me a little thrill. I can't abide the thought of two women in bed, but two hairy men—delicious."

"I guess we have a lot in common, then."

Juno laughed, and I asked her again what she thought of White Studies, perhaps because I got a charge out of seeing her angry.

"It'll never happen," she assured me. "Never. Never even get off the ground."

I was about to ask her how she could be so certain when a creepy silence greeted Dean and Nina Bullerschmidt's arrival. Even the piano music stopped. While the dean loitered at the door as if awaiting a trumpet fanfare or a rolled-out carpet, Nina rushed over to Cypriani to rave about her "gown." The dean eyed everything in the room as if assessing its value, and everyone in the room as if wishing them harm.

I turned away, wandering off into a small study to check out what Cypriani was reading. This is a bad habit of mine, and Stefan will often drag me from bookshelves at a party—but silent communion with books can often be more entertaining than talking to their owners.

I didn't learn much in this grandly bland little room, except that the extra-wide armchairs were very comfortable and could almost seat two people each. Aside from a newsstand's worth of newspapers and magazines that included everything from the *New York Review of Books* and the *Economist* to the *Wine Enthusiast* and *Travel and Leisure*, the only books in sight were Cypriani's own, in multiple copies, obviously meant to be used as gifts—or weapons? Surely she read something else?

Bill and Betty Malatesta found me there, and I saw at once that the usually cool couple was very much on edge. They held hands—*clutched* was more like it—as if restraining themselves from violence. They said hi and took everything in with open envy, which disappointed me. Most graduate students learn to frame their envy as admiration, and the Malatestas had led the pack. But then their job searches had faltered and failed, and their performances had suffered.

Bill let go Betty's hand. "How many White Studies profs does it take to change a lightbulb?" he asked, and I was pleased he was back to this running series of jokes.

"I'm stumped."

"What lightbulb? Hey, are we outa Buds?"

I grinned. "That's good."

"I've got a better one. How much money does it take to support an endowed chair?" He answered before I could even blink: "If you have to ask, you can't afford one."

Betty chuckled like Kathy Bates in *Misery*, and I watched the Malatestas head off and attempt to chat up Cypriani. They might not have thought much of her, but she could have connections that could prove useful. Curious, I followed them. Betty was commenting about Toni Morrison's new book and asked if Cypriani knew her.

"I know everyone," Camille snapped. "Whether I want to or not. And Toni's a lush," she added. Without prompting, she went on to defame every writer Betty and Bill mentioned as either a drunkard, impotent, or washed-up. Saul Bellow? "A total cunt." She made these assertions with such sullen authority, they sounded absolutely true—but how could they be? "Salman Rushdie shouldn't be the only one with a death threat." Her vociferous delivery carried mad conviction and magnetized the room as everyone drew in closer to hear her slime other writers.

Suddenly Camille launched into a bizarre anecdote. "Let me tell you about how I. B. Singer was so drunk he almost knocked me off a platform at a writer's conference! We were in Barcelona—"

Bill interrupted her. "This story sounds too good to be true."

Camille froze. "It's not a story," she said coldly. "I write stories, I don't tell them. And who the hell are you, anyway?" It wasn't quite the moment in a movie saloon where the villain walks through the swinging doors, but it was close, and the freaky evening seemed to be spinning out of control. Camille tromped into the kitchen, and Betty nabbed Bill and started bitching him out in a harsh whisper.

As the crowd of gawking spectators broke into smaller groups, Juno popped up behind me and said, "Exactly which circle of hell do you think we're in right now?"

Startled by the reference, I looked blank.

"Hell has to be seeing Dean Bullerschmidt every two days," Juno continued. "Don't you think?"

"Then why did you come?"

Juno grinned. "Because I love an occasion." She whirled around like a model, and I said, "You *are* an occasion." And at that moment it was as if the whole experience in the pool had never happened, and I could see Juno totally from outside, as a spectacle. I enjoyed her, without being moved and disturbed.

Sharon walked over, and having heard this last interchange, she applauded. After quick introductions, the two women moved off to chat—apparently about each other's clothes and hair, from what I could make out. But I was jarred by Juno's reference to hell. Could Juno, who Stefan thought was wild and unstable, actually be persecuting me and slyly referring to Dante? But what for? What the hell for? What would she be getting out of it? It just didn't add up.

Stefan appeared with rum and Cokes for both of us, explaining that he'd been snooping in the other rooms. "Her stuff must be back East. This place is just a sweater she can slip on."

I sipped my drink gratefully. "It may be a sweater, but it's cashmere. With a Tiffany's sweater guard." Without saying anything about my attraction to Juno, I pulled Stefan aside and relayed our little interaction and my suspicions.

"Nick, Juno could probably burn down a mailbox just for fun, or a dare, or because it felt sexy. But leaving a Penguin paperback in your office mailbox? Too subtle."

"That's what I think."

The noise level had risen around us with the alcohol consumption, and the dean, Cypriani, Serena, and Nina were now clustered in one corner in replay of the dean's reception, while various levels of toadying swirled around them. I watched Nina gaze from Camille to the dean with Nancy Reagan eyes and felt my hands go cold. I remembered the scene in *Desperately Seeking Susan* where Madonna reads Rosanna Arquette's diary and snaps, "This has to be code—nobody's life could be this boring." Nina was so innocuous, so sweet. Little Miss Evil?

I thought of my stupid confrontation with the dean last year. What if Nina had decided to take revenge on me? What would be cannier than waiting a few months or more? And who would suspect this demure, harmless administrator's wife of a tiny terror campaign? The dean wouldn't have had to put her up to it —the same wild loyalty that made her worship Camille Cypriani probably tied her to the dean and would make her want to defend him. If I was right, the question then was: How far would she go?

"The Forum," Stefan said.

"What?"

"Julius Caesar. Can't you see Camille surrounded by people with knives? Sinking in a sea of blood."

The pianist started playing—of all things—"The House of the Rising Sun." It took me a moment to switch gears from brooding about Nina Bullerschmidt and concentrate on what Stefan had suggested. "Is that a vision, or a fantasy?"

"Haven't you ever thought of it? I mean, look at the murderers we've met since coming to SUM. They're not on TV, they're right here, people we know. They seemed normal enough, but they got pushed too far. We seem normal, too, but—"

"Don't even joke about killing someone—that's a terrible mistake. What if people overheard you?"

"You think I care anymore?" He shook his head bitterly, downing half of his drink. "For the sake of poetic reference, it should be Cash who strikes the first blow, since there may be plenty of brutes in EAR, but there's no Brutus."

I couldn't tell if Stefan's comments were fueled by depression, bravado, or sick humor, but I didn't like it at all, and I waved Sharon over. But before I could enlist her support, Dean Bullerschmidt called for quiet. He got it.

With his orotund, low voice and unctuous manner, he could have been a nineteenth-century Central European mayor greeting a royal couple he loathed but had to welcome with poetry and praise. "I'd like to announce that Camille Cypriani, the newest and most valued addition to the College of Arts and Letters, has graciously and gracefully agreed to chair the College's Task Force exploring the creation of a White Studies Program."

Betty Malatesta pivoted away from the drinks table, spilling her wine. The news had somehow not yet reached the TAs, or at least her. Betty's surprise told me how out of the loop she had become at EAR, and that probably made her angry.

"What?" she spat. "White Studies! You guys aren't funding the programs you *do* have, and you're going to add some bullshit racist propaganda passing itself off as a legitimate field of inquiry?"

"She must have been clipping articles, too," Stefan whispered to me. Bill tried shushing her, but Betty wouldn't stop berating the dean. "You can't possibly support anything so bogus and anti-intellectual."

Cash Jurevicius chimed in: "It's disgraceful for Arts and Letters to even consider such a program. You're betraying my grandmother's ideals. You don't care about anything human or decent or fine," he said, and there was some surreptitious applause from people out of the dean's line of sight. "You've torn apart my grandmother's library. That was her office—that was her legacy to SUM. She loved this school, she loved the students, but you're all hypocrites. And you've defiled her office by putting a has-been and a fraud in there."

"You lousy sonofabitch!" Camille howled, pitching her empty whiskey glass at Cash. She was bracing herself to go for blood when she was held back by the amazingly strong Bullerschmidt, who just then looked as if he could have tossed her in the air and juggled with her.

"That's it for me," Stefan said, and he hustled us to the door like a Secret Service agent rushing his president away from gunfire. Outside he said, "Maybe they'll all just kill each other in there and we can start over."

We drove home quietly after that comment, Sharon expressing her surprise in occasional bursts of disbelief. "How can people be as bitter as they are? So mean?"

"Well," I said, "look at the up side. If outbursts like this become the norm at EAR functions, the parties are at least gonna be more entertaining. And then we also have a built-in excuse to leave early."

"How can you make a joke about it?" Sharon asked.

"There's nothing left but laughing at it."

Stefan agreed. "Nick is right. This place has exhausted every other possible response."

"Don't be so sure," Sharon warned. "That crew back there didn't look like they'd be watching Comedy Central any time soon."

11

I DREAMED that night not about Manderley, but a doughnut shop. I woke up well before morning with the aroma of something baking wafting up from the kitchen, so I headed downstairs and found Sharon reading *Vogue* and waiting for the oven timer to buzz.

"I couldn't sleep," she explained. "I brewed some decaf and decided to bake some mocha brownies. Baking soothes me." She showed me the recipe, one she had clipped from *Saveur* and brought with her.

"Yum." The recipe called for brewed coffee, ground coffee, *and* instant coffee.

I shuffled over to the table and sat by her. Even with insomnia, she looked good, in slightly oversize azure silk pajamas that gave her a very 1930s air. Sharon poured me a cup of coffee and we took turns licking the batter out of the mixing bowl while we waited for the brownies to be done. We talked about White Studies, SUM politics, and Stefan's moodiness, failing career, and possible chances for some reversal of fortune. It's not that we hadn't discussed these topics before, but we were like that couple in Henry James's *The Ambassadors*, who were so close that "the circle in which they stood was bright with life and every question lived there as nowhere else."

"You know, Nick, honestly, I wonder if SUM just isn't the completely wrong place for you and Stefan. A wrong turn in the road. As much as you like Michigan—and your place up north when you get to it . . . Look at how painful life has been here for him, and for you. I know it hasn't always been like that, it's not nonstop, but you never dealt with being threatened or beaten up when you were in New York or Massachusetts. Nobody burned your mailbox. You were never a murder suspect—and you never saw a corpse before except on the news."

"It's all true."

"Do you mind my saying that?"

"I've been asking myself the same things lately, about this place, but it doesn't get me anywhere. Stefan's damned lucky he was chosen for the writer-in-residence slot when he was. Those positions are plums, and right now, five years later, he's not successful enough anymore to move someplace else. So he's got the job for life. And if I got tenure and promotion, we'd be set."

"Set for what? Crazy colleagues? Intellectual fraud? Drowning in hypocrisy? The occasional murder?"

"It's a life," I argued.

"For how long?"

"It's a life," I repeated.

"Sweetie, you are in denial."

"This is not denial—it's a postponement."

She stared down into her mug.

"Sharon, I hate academia, but I love teaching. I love working with students. I know it's not exactly the Peace Corps or UNICEF, but what I do does change the world a little, just a little. Isn't that important?"

"I know it's important, but is it safe, is it healthy here for you? I don't get it. Your colleagues don't respect you because you're just a bibliographer—you've been telling me that since you got here. As an archivist, I think your work's much more important than the average academic tome, but so what? I'm not voting on your tenure, and I'm not here working with you."

"Does anyone get respect at work?"

"I do, at Columbia. People take me seriously."

I wondered if the glamorous modeling career she'd had before going back to school and becoming an archivist might not have something to do with that—the money she'd earned, the celebrity, and her looks and style, too. She had been able to change careers because she'd left school unfinished when she started modeling full-time, and always regretted it. But me, I was living my dream, there wasn't anything else I wanted to do.

"Sharon, Columbia University, that's not the real world. It's easy to tell me to leave, but how could we? Stefan's stepmother gave us that great cabin up north, and look at this house—it's terrific." Even as I said that, I knew that people sold houses all the time and moved, and that five years wasn't necessarily enough time to feel rooted.

"Sure, it's a great house—until someone burns it down."

I must have looked very ugly then, because Sharon immediately apologized for the remark. Then I apologized.

"But you haven't done anything," she said, wearily shaking her head and clasping my hands in hers. "I was the one who was out of line." She let go of my hands gently.

I wanted to say that I should have been more understanding of her nerves, but I didn't want to patronize her. I knew Sharon was worried about the upcoming surgeon's appointment on Monday.

As if she were following my thoughts, she started talking about it. "This doctor may be a midwesterner and educated at the Mayo Clinic, but let me tell you, honey, he doesn't act any more human than the surgeons in New York and Boston that I've consulted. You should see the people around him—disciples, groupies practically. It bothers me to feel like Cinderella begging to go to the ball. And I wish he was older," she sighed. "He's just too smart and good-looking and famous in his field. I don't think he knows what it's like to be afraid. I honestly don't think he's suffered. I saw the pictures on his desk—beautiful wife, beautiful kids. A dog—country home—a boat!"

"How can you tell he hasn't suffered?"

"I just feel it. He's so smug."

The phone rang, startling both of us, but when I grabbed it, there was just a click, a strange click, and a mechanical hiss.

"What?" Sharon asked, reading my face when I set down the receiver, shaking my head.

"Don't laugh. It sounded, well, it sounded like a cigarette lighter. Remember the last note I got? It read, Next time it could be you. This was the next warning."

"Nick, how could you tell *anything* about the call? It's so late—you're tired and upset. Are you sure?"

I nodded, wishing we had caller ID, but convinced that whoever was behind this harassment would have blocked it or used a public phone. "I thought it was over. I don't know why. But I did. I thought when nothing happened today that—"

"—you were safe? I don't think we're ever safe. We just think we are. And every now and then something happens that makes it clear. Remember that line Stefan found someplace?"

I nodded, and quoted from a Polish Jewish writer I'd never heard of before until Stefan had told me about him, and whose name I always forgot: "Behind the stage of our life, concealed in the wings, great factories of suffering are at work."

"Right now they're working overtime for you guys."

"But things have to change," I said, not convincing myself. Even a brownie didn't help, despite being hot and rich and sweet.

I kissed and hugged Sharon good night, hoping she'd be able to sleep at least a little, and headed back to bed. I lay there for a while, hoping too that I'd imagined the sound of the lighter, hoping it was a wrong number. Something. Anything.

And then I idly found myself wishing I were back in that five-year period in which the thing that mattered most in the world was doing my Wharton bibliography. Life was ordered then, life had structure, life made sense. I lived in a welter of reading, photocopying, correspondence, filing, annotating. Nothing really touched me then. Nothing hurt. Because I was too freaked out by the amount of work, the piles of photocopies, the constant record-keeping. It was armor—it was a crutch—it was a nightmare.

In the morning I felt the almost physical sense of oppression you get before a huge thunderstorm. At breakfast with Stefan and Sharon, I openly shared my sense of looming disaster. There was nothing either one of them could say that could dispel my dark thoughts.

But Stefan said I had to be wrong about the phone call. "Nick, how could you know that specifically it was a lighter? You were nervous, you heard something." He shrugged, "Besides, how do you know it was for us or for you? Remember that year we used to get phone calls for some Debbie? And that month when the fax rang once at about five in the afternoon every other day but never connected?"

After breakfast, I headed to campus for my mail, not even troubled by the ranks of students, the darting bicyclists, the traffic, the noise and commotion. On the second floor, though, I found trouble.

There was an enormous EAR sign opposite the stairs, with every professor's name spelled out in plastic letters in horizontal grooves, accompanied by the office number. In that vast field of white on black, the letters for my name were discolored. As I leaned forward I saw that they were charred and brown, melted, dripping and drooping like rock poster letters did in the 1960s. I stared at them, feeling numb. Nobody else's name had been messed with. This was another message.

In the office, I complained to Dulcie Halligan, who looked only superficially upset when she promised to have the letters replaced as soon as she could get to it. I think she was enjoying my discomfiture, as if it were appropriate payback for having raised my voice and banged the office door the other day. Could she really be that petty? Yes, because she had the nerve to ask, "You're sure they're not just worn out, Professor?"

She wasn't the only one who could be small. "Dulcie, I graduated college *summa* cum laude. Yes, I'm sure."

It worked. She whirled away from me as if I'd spit at her. It was a cheap victory that I would eventually pay for, since even I knew that alienating a secretary was never a bright idea. But I had a big mouth. I was quip-happy. Call it what you like, it meant trouble.

With this cheerful experience behind me, I grabbed my mail and descended to Parker's foul-smelling basement, which was quiet just then. But there was something different and disgusting in the air—not roach spray, or leaking sewage pipes, or mold from the boiler room. Fire? I didn't see any smoke, yet I tensed up.

The plastic nameplate on my office door had been ripped off, and the door itself was as open as Oprah talking about her dysfunctions. And not just open. When I stepped closer I saw that it had been *broken* open. The lock was twisted and scarred, the splintered frame around it looking almost bitten or chewed on. Someone had used a crowbar or a mallet and chisel to break into my office. But there was nothing valuable there—what could they be after?

I stood there, staring, unable to enter the moment. It was so unreal, something out of a book or film, surely not my own life.

The thick overvarnished door looked otherwise untouched. With the building pulsing quietly around me, I set down my briefcase and approached. The smell of something burned was stronger now. Did I expect to see someone lurking inside? Or a whirlwind of destruction? I wasn't sure. I stood at the ruined doorway looking in, and there was nothing changed, nothing moved or disrupted—except my round black metal wastebasket. It was a few inches out from the side of my desk instead of right next to it.

Students passed by outside my office, their legs revealed up to their shins through the weird, barred half-window. Preternaturally quiet myself now, I could hear Parker's plumbing, the 150-year-old building's general creaks and groans, and what might be rats in the thick walls.

Stepping back into the hallway, I scooped up my briefcase and went back into my violated office. There was no ghost there, yet it felt haunted by someone's rage. And when I peered at last down into the wastebasket, I couldn't help gasping since I recognized its contents instantly—as I was meant to, of course.

It was a charred copy of my Wharton bibliography, and I picked it up mournfully, tenderly, as if it might cry out in pain. I opened the blistered, blackened cover and leafed through the thick book. Someone had very deliberately burned the title page so that my name was destroyed, and then singed and scorched most of the rest of the pages. With a kind of furious objectivity, I studied the damage, guessing that it was done with one of those fire starters like the kind Stefan and I used to light Shabbat candles at home.

This felt even more personal than the mailbox, and I sat down heavily with the smoked, ravaged book in my hands, thinking about my conversation with Sharon in the middle of the night, and her urging me to leave. Was that the aim of all this? Did someone want to drive me from EAR? Whom had I threatened? I was powerless, I wasn't anyone's rival.

I looked up the number, called Detective Valley of SUM's Campus Police, and said it was urgent—I was being harassed, and my office had been broken into and vandalized. Then I called upstairs to report what had happened and that we needed a locksmith to put in a new lock and arrange for new keys.

"Not your day, is it?" Dulcie Halligan asked primly, as if I were an errant politician reeling from one scandal to another.

Then I called home to tell Stefan, who responded to the bad news with a tenor, "Shit, what next?"

"Don't say that!" I warned superstitiously. Stefan called Sharon to the phone, and both of them tried to soothe me, but they both sounded as shell-shocked as I was. Yes, it was only a book that had been damaged, but it was *my* book, the only one I'd published so far, and it represented not merely hundreds of hours of research. It had grown out of my love of Edith Wharton's fiction, it was my offering to the world. Maybe not as grand as a painting or a symphony, but it was something I had created. A legacy.

After I hung up, I did what I should have done right away: combed through my files, examined my desk, inspected every square inch of the room to see if anything had been stolen or tampered with. But the office was amazingly, almost mockingly untouched.

Valley showed up quicker than I expected he would to inspect the damage, but he was brutally annoyed that there was nothing more to look at.

"You said vandalized."

It came out like a dull accusation, but then this redheaded Ichabod Crane in his Kmart blue suit could make me feel defensive just by saying hello. I had been on his shit list for a few years now, ever since being one of the last people to see a murder victim alive. Further involvement with murders had done nothing to change his opinion of me. But he probably also knew that I thought him faintly ridiculous despite his status as the sole legal authority on campus, and he resented it.

"Look at the door—look at this book! Isn't this vandalism?"

But he had looked, and he was not impressed. "Did you know people toss couches out of dorm windows on campus? Set trees on fire? Trees. Drive their cars over bikes? Rip STOP signs out of the ground and throw them into the river? Knock over light poles? Attack dorm washers and dryers with hammers and drills? Piss on computers in the library and short them out?"

"You don't care about what happened to me."

He frowned. "Nothing's missing, nothing's damaged? Then one book and one door isn't a whole lot to get excited about."

"But it's my door and my book!"

"Uh-huh."

"You're saying it's my fault?"

"All I said was 'uh-huh.' You want to talk to my superior?" He told me he was going to file a report and then turned to go.

"Wait!" Valley had never thought much of me or EAR or any faculty members, and I could see our stock plummet even further as I unleashed a torrent of details about the other incidents and the current climate in EAR.

This seemed to get Valley's attention. "You think this could be about your vote in an election that hasn't been held yet—or because some other professor hates your guts? Am I getting that right?"

I tried explaining the passions that can create pyroclastic flow in EAR without even a warning rumble, but Valley was dubious. "Why should anyone want to mess with you?" he asked. "Shouldn't that woman, Katherine, Clarice—"

"Camille."

"Shouldn't she be the target since she's so controversial, if you're right? How come nobody's bugging her?"

"I'm not being bugged—I'm being stalked." His lack of interest was driving me to hyperbole. Valley blinked. "Well, almost. And are you saying I'm the one behind this? That I'm crying wolf?"

"No. But you raised it," Valley replied coolly. "And you think your hearing's good enough to detect the sound of a lighter over the phone." His scorn made me waver. Maybe I'd just been hallucinating. "And why concentrate on a professor suspect anyway? What about your students? There was one last year who didn't like you much."

"He's dead. Besides, I have terrific student evaluations! They all think I'm great!" Even as I said it, I knew it was an exaggeration, but at this point I couldn't imagine a student going to so much trouble. Besides, it would take mature, mean wit to think of the Dante book and all the fires. That struck me as too subtle for most undergraduates.

Valley shrugged.

"So you won't take *any* action?"

"Listen, the Michiganapolis Police are the ones who have jurisdiction over the arson at your house, and like I said, a burned book and a busted door is pretty insignificant property damage on campus compared to what goes on most of the time. It'll be reported, but that's it."

"You're not taking this seriously," I said.

"Nobody's been hurt, nothing's been stolen, damage is minor."

"So you'll only pay attention if they blow up my office or I get beaten up or killed here."

"That would do it," Valley said on the way out. "Definitely." And out in the hallway, he added, "You know, maybe someone just hates your *name*."

With Valley gone, I couldn't believe that I had missed the obvious connection myself. My *name* was connected to almost every episode: campus mailbox, home mailbox, EAR sign, office nameplate, title page of my book. But then I drooped. So what? What did it mean? Nothing.

Well, so much for wanting to move from the third floor because of painful memories up there. I might as well have stayed and hired a bodyguard if trouble was just going to follow me to the basement, or bought an alarm system for the office.

But I couldn't just sit there and wait for the next blow, even if Detective Valley was unconcerned and the Michiganapolis police hadn't reported any progress on the arson investigation.

I dug out a yellow legal pad to jot things down. Suspects, suspects. I'd been at this place before, though the surroundings were always more salubrious and encouraged ratiocination. But the good side was that here, I was trying to figure out a lesser crime than murder. That had to be a change for the better, taking the long view of my years at SUM.

If there had only been the one incident with our mailbox at home, I might have been able to settle down eventually and assume it was indeed rowdy teenagers or even drunken frat boys playing a prank, and maybe even a rogue anti-Semite, as terrible as that was to contemplate. But with half a dozen strikes at me, this wasn't remotely random.

Somebody was pissed off at me and making a real effort to show it. Who? Why? Or should I just list everyone suspicious and try to sort it out that way? The week had been so shadowed by Sharon's visit, by the hubbub of the semester starting and the more than usual academic craziness, that I hadn't been at all systematic in my thinking.

I started with Serena. She'd been very cold to me lately. Could there be something more going on than just her newly acquired administrative hauteur? Could she resent my growing friendship with Juno and even suspect I might vote for the more flamboyant candidate? After all, Serena had shared many dyspeptic observations about the EAR department with me before, so she must be aware that faculty might vote for Juno out of sheer perversity or a desire to strike out at whomever they identified as their enemies. Serena herself had never been entirely popular, and as the former chair of Rhetoric, she carried a stigma she was terribly aware of. Get her talking, and she could make herself and the Rhetoric faculty sound like Kosovars.

Then there was Juno herself, though if she was coming on to me at one moment and setting fires to freak me out at another, she had some serious issues with ambivalence. Still, she was incendiary, and she had called herself "a mean bitch." But to be fair, she'd explained she would never do anything underhanded to revenge herself on a person, and all these acts had been anonymous. Wouldn't Juno want credit?

Iris and Carter had been pressuring and even threatening me in various ways about my tenure review and the election, but would they actually have the nerve to do more than mouth off at people? On the other hand, they had been desperately unhappy in EAR for decades, so who knew what might set them off and who might be their target? What if they envied me because even though my status was low, Stefan's was not? It was a loony reason to take after me, but teaching classes you hate in a department that sneered at you could twist anyone's psyche after a few decades.

Granting that, I still dismissed the wild suggestion Stefan made about Cypriani setting fire to our mailbox. She had too much to lose at SUM by causing any more than emotional trouble; her position was so cushy and remunerative. She may have stomped on Stefan's ego with that caustic note, but why bother with him anymore, and why target me, too?

But Summerscale appeared to be a very likely suspect; he was so intemperate, and he seemed to think I was a jerk. Now he was someone I could imagine plotting down in this basement like the Phantom of the Opera out to destroy everyone who had humiliated him. And he had easy access, since he was just down the hall, and could have probably broken in my office door without tools. Picturing him on a rampage, I regretted nervously making light of our basement offices. Still, it was really the provost and the dean who had felled him, not me.

Moving higher up the ladder, there was always our august dean, who must still resent me for my intrusion into his home last year in an attempt to solve a murder. I grimaced at the memory, at having suspected him of the killing. With a man as coldhearted as that, it was easy to picture him taking insidious revenge. And since the dean was so recognizable, he might even have hired someone to do it for him. Or it could have been the dean working together with Nina, unless she had become Cat Lady all by herself. The dean wasn't averse to misusing his influence with graduate students—so what if he was somehow manipulating one of the impecunious TAs?

And they might have it in for me on their own. After all, my move down to the basement had displaced Betty and Bill, who as senior teaching assistants must have relished an office that wasn't as overcrowded as the other TA offices down there. And they'd been so bitter since their job searches last year hadn't led to tenure-track teaching posts. What if this thuggery was letting off steam for them as well as striking out? The Modern Language Association often offered panels about alternative employment for graduate students; maybe they should add low-level crime and intimidation.

Closer to home, there was the hugely disappointed Didier, who had hopes of enormous success and best-sellerdom. Now he'd been shunted aside by his publisher, whose treatment of Didier sent the message that they regretted having purchased his book in the first place. Didier had been drinking heavily, so maybe he'd done things he wasn't fully aware of. But the problem with Didier, though, was that though he could get onto campus like anyone else, since there's no real security and he could swipe Lucille's keys, why would he bother? Why not target someone in publishing if he was vengeful? After all, Stefan wasn't having any luck with his career either, and taking it out on me hurt Stefan, too. Didier may have been gruff, but he'd never seemed cruel. Wasn't there some kind of weight lifter's code anyway? Something that enjoined you from setting fires on someone who spotted for you at the gym?

I hated to ask myself this question, since she had helped us, but what about New Age-y Polly down the street, who had called the police about the burning mailbox? She claimed to have felt vibrations the night of the arson, but what if she set the fire herself because some spirit urged her on, or because the act had ritual, mystical significance? Maybe our spaced-out neighbor was signaling aliens to come take her away. Maybe she just wanted to feel important—or what if she had some weird crush on one of us and wanted to play rescuer?

Looking over my notes, I felt a sense of frustration and emptiness, recalling Inspector Clouseau's silly comment, "I suspect everyone—and I suspect no one." All of these people could be responsible, but it was just as likely that none of them were.

12

WITH that cheerful realization, I got ready to troop off to teach. Just then someone in green overalls and jangling tool belt from the physical plant showed up to repair the door, accompanied by Dulcie Halligan, who stood there surveying the damage as if it were not just my fault, but an indication of some deep corruption on my part.

"Thanks for your help," I threw off as I left.

"They don't care," I heard her saying to the carpenter guy.

What the hell did that mean?

Despite this send-off, I felt useful and competent in class, and that was despite the fact that we met in Uplegger Hall. This was an older building near Parker that had recently been retrofitted, which meant it now had harsh lighting and far too many uncomfortable seats in each room. Lab rats had it only slightly better than students and professors did in this hall, which is probably why the faceless minions-in-charge-of-scheduling had moved so many EAR classes there. Maybe they hoped for mass faculty psychosis, resignations, and retirements so they could hire people at minimum academic wage to teach writing, that pariah course.

Leaving Uplegger, I saw a miscellaneous small group of students headed toward the Administration Building, carrying well-made picket signs that read WHITE STUDIES–RACISM and SUM HATES MINORITIES. So, word was out and the protests had started. How ugly would it get?

Back home after class, I found Sharon musing out in the sun room, with a Modern Library copy of *Mrs. Dalloway* in her lap. We hugged, and she played with my hair before I sat down next to her.

"I was just thinking of that book yesterday," I marveled, but then we'd often felt connected in unseen ways.

"I love reading this," she said. "It's so beautiful it can break your heart."

"Absolutely. Her prose is sometimes half poetry, half prayer."

"Have you ever thought of doing a bibliography of Woolf?"

"I get invitations all the time to do different writers for different presses, but one is enough. I wouldn't put myself—or Stefan—through that again. It was my version of *Mr. Blandings Builds His Dream House.*"

Sharon nodded, and we were soon talking about her surgery.

"Nick, it's so invasive, and the side effects—! I've been reading everything I can find, and it's not good news. People in my situation sometimes have spinal fluid leaks, and there's a strong risk of meningitis, which can kill you if they don't catch it quick enough. It's not like Bette Davis climbing onto the bed in *Dark Victory*, she pets the dogs and the angels sing her to sleep. Even the anesthesia is dangerous—people can die just from being put under."

"And your parents wanted you to hurry up."

"If I had, I wouldn't know how much risk was involved. But now . . ." She was despondent and dazed.

"Would it cheer you up at all to contemplate who might be harassing me? I know we've talked about it before, but maybe this time we'll see what we missed."

Sharon smiled. "I'll play Nancy Drew with you, but first I

need a drink. And so do you, after what happened today." Sharon led me to the kitchen. "I am going to make you a Rampage. Friends from Vancouver taught me how: champagne, bitters, red vermouth, slices of orange and cucumber. You have all that, don't you?"

I pointed to various parts of the kitchen while Sharon busied herself. "Do you think people did this when Sarajevo was under siege?"

"Made drinks or made jokes?"

"Both, I guess."

"If you can, why choose not to?"

The Rampage was very good when she was done. "But the name. Rampage is not an image you think of when it comes to Canadians," I said, remembering a Mavis Gallant story about embarrassed Canadians in a movie theater. "They all ooh and aah when they see this puppy, but then they gasp because they've expressed emotion in public. It's devastating."

"What about Juno Dromgoole? She's pretty damned rampageous. Do you still have the hots for her?"

"It wasn't a twenty-four-hour flu," I replied with dignity. "Of course I do, I think. But I don't want to deal with that right now, it's too confusing and weird."

I retrieved my pad with the list of suspects and ran through them for Sharon, who listened thoughtfully. When I was done, she said with no hesitation, "Cut Polly Flockhart."

"Why?"

"From how you've described her before, she's too spaced out to cause real trouble. She'd get a voodoo doll or cemetery dust or light black candles against you. What's been happening is too practical, too real."

"But what if she was in a trance state? Or channeling a Visigoth in the mood to sack?"

"I vote for Byron Summerscale, because he's been so humiliated. If shame made Germany go to war, it could turn a Humanities professor into the Terminator."

"But why me?" I wanted to know. "Why hassle *me*? Summerscale should be going after administrators—they're the ones who've been screwing him over for years."

"You're a convenient target, since you're right there in the Parker Hall basement, and you did treat him badly."

"It was a joke. I was trying to cheer him up."

"It's only a joke if somebody thinks it's funny, and he wasn't laughing, was he? He called you, what, a Philistine?"

"By implication, since he's Samson. No, he said worse things than that—he called me a stooge, and other stuff—" I tried recalling what else he'd said, and couldn't. Either I was becoming inured to it all after so much, or I was losing my grip.

"This isn't going to get us very far, Nick. Why don't you do what Hercule Poirot always does—bring everyone together in one place and bully or trick the culprit into confessing?"

"That would really make me popular," I said sourly. "And why would any of the suspects agree to gather?"

"You could do it here, have a reception or something, tomorrow night, even, since it's the weekend, and say it's in honor of Camille. How could they stay away if everyone's sucking up to her? Camille would come, wouldn't she? And then everyone else would feel obliged to."

"Are you serious?"

"Possibly."

"Stefan would choke at the idea."

"You know, Stefan might be grateful. He could always use it as material for a book."

"We've been through this before. He's not wild about mysteries or thrillers, with only one exception. He loves Jean-Claude Van Damme—but only in that hockey movie *Sudden Death*."

"Oh, I saw that on cable. There's not much chance of a chase scene or explosions or a plane crash with your crew," Sharon observed. "But they're spicy enough as it is, don't you think?"

Sharon's suggestion had retriggered all my anxiety about Stefan. I felt utterly powerless to help him, more than ever before, and Stefan was making it worse by shutting me out. "His career is like the *Titanic*, honey, and he's just barely hanging on.

It's killing him to see people he knew in graduate school doing better than he is. And then, the whole country's filled with lousy writers making it big."

"Isn't that how it works? Couldn't he write a big fat crummy book that would earn him a lot of money and shut him up?"

Before I could figure out how to reply, Stefan walked into the kitchen looking very strange. I assumed that he'd received even more bad news from his agent or something else had happened to deepen his despair about his career, though what could be next?

"Stefan, can I make you a Rampage?" Sharon explained what it was, but Stefan said he wasn't mixing his champagne with anything. He poured himself a glass from the bottle on ice. I thought, God, this is so *Dynasty*.

Stefan said, "I have some news."

Sharon and I both asked, "What?"

"Camille Cypriani is dead." And he gave me a smile as sharp as an ice pick, then wagged his eyebrows like Groucho Marx.

My first terrible thought was that Stefan had flipped out and killed her. I could see Stefan finding the chance to run her over in the parking lot and gunning his engine. Or walking behind her on a staircase and giving her a hard shove. And from Sharon's disbelieving, watchful expression, I could tell something similar was going through her mind. We waited for Stefan to explain. I hoped that I was wrong, and even that Stefan was wrong, too. Somehow.

Expressionless, Stefan said, "I was in my office at Parker. I heard a phone ring and ring down the hall, endlessly, where Camille's office is. Then one of the EAR secretaries came out of the main office, her heels echoing. You know how noisy it can be there with those high ceilings," he said, and I nodded.

"Then someone screamed. When I rushed into the hall, I could see Dulcie Halligan backing away from Camille's office door. She kind of fell into my arms and started sobbing. She said she'd gone down to Cypriani's office, because she knew Camille was in but wasn't answering the phone."

"Her office was open?" I asked. "I mean the department door? It's usually closed, isn't it?"

Stefan nodded. "Somebody had made a delivery and left it propped open. Camille's door was apparently closed, but unlocked, and when Dulcie opened it, she saw Camille sprawled back in her desk chair, dead."

"Are you positive?" I asked.

Smiling again, he said, "I saw enough to be sure, Nick. I didn't let Dulcie go back inside, but you could tell even standing at the doorway. Camille's dead, Nick. Dead, dead, dead. No mistake. Her face was sort of blue—her tongue was sticking out —there was a scarf around her neck. Why bother checking her pulse?" He shrugged blithely. "It was pretty obvious somebody had strangled her good." And now he grinned, and Sharon walked over to hug him—or calm him down? "I guess an endowed chair wasn't the best career move she could have made," Stefan noted, shaking his head, his eyes glowing with surprise and delight.

Her chair, I thought, struck by something that teased at me, half-formed, but wouldn't appear.

"What was she wearing?" Sharon asked, letting him go.

"Sharon!" I couldn't believe she'd ask that.

But she persisted: "I want to picture it."

Stefan described some kind of satiny-looking suit that seemed brocaded.

"Sounds like another Oscar de la Renta," she said thoughtfully. "I know that suit. What color? Beige? Really?" She shook her head. "Not a good color for her."

"She's dead," I pointed out. "Does it matter?"

"If you wear designer clothes it *always* matters."

I was full of my own questions for Stefan: Who else was on the scene? Did the emergency medical service come? What about the campus police?

Now Stefan was really wound up. "Valley asked me where *you* were! I guess it's not an official murder at SUM unless Nick Hoffman is involved. But you'll see it on the news at six." Then he listed everyone he saw there, and it was a sizable group:

Serena Fisch and Bullerschmidt, who'd been having a meeting with her; the EAR office staff; the Malatestas and Summerscale from downstairs; Cash Jurevicius, who came out of the EAR office; Iris and Carter; Juno. "It was a mob scene. I gave Valley a short statement and told him he could find me at home if he wanted more. He was more interested in Dulcie, though."

"Stefan, did you notice anything about the people who were there?" Sharon asked, on the trail. "Was there anything striking or out of place?"

Stefan had some more champagne. "I guess at some level, they were all ghoulishly fascinated by what happened as much as shocked. I know I was." He closed his eyes to recall more, and seemed to be writing the scene for us. "The Malatestas were at the edge of the crowd, you know, like they thought someone might ask them to leave because they didn't belong there since they're only TAs. They didn't used to be like that." He paused. "Serena and the dean had sort of grave, officially shocked looks, hard to read. The secretaries, they were thrilled, except for Dulcie. She was shaky and pale. Juno looked annoyed. Incredulous. And she said a few things about how violent Americans were and how this would never happen in Canada, ever."

Sharon and I grinned, and I said, "That must have gone over well with the spectators, and Valley."

"Summerscale had a wrath-of-God face," Stefan continued, concentrating. "But he blows up like a storm at anything, so that's not unusual. Cash looked mean and weasely and deprived, as usual."

Sharon objected, "But he's cute."

Stefan said, "You've been around all the gays in New York for too long if you think *he's* cute."

"Get back to the story," I urged, not wanting to argue about Cash's looks.

"Okay. Iris and Carter were lurking at the fringes as quietly as those spiders that dig pits and wait for the prey to tumble in."

Sharon made a face at that. I guess she didn't enjoy the Discovery channel.

"It's got to be Dulcie," I said. "She's always so arrogant and defensive, thinks people put on airs and disrespect her."

"And?" Stefan asked.

"It's obvious, isn't it? She killed Camille, and then pretended to discover the body. It's perfect. It happens all the time in books. She couldn't stand seeing a woman her age be so successful when she's just a secretary. She's always complaining that people don't treat her well even though she has a B.A. and graduated cum laude."

Stefan completely discounted that. "Just because it happens in books doesn't make it obvious. In fact, it makes it a hundred times less likely."

"Are all these people getting murdered at SUM likely?" Sharon wondered.

"Good point," I said.

Stefan went on, "Besides, Dulcie's too self-centered to kill anyone."

I thought about it, and reluctantly agreed.

Sharon asked, "What happens to the endowed chair now?"

Stefan clapped his hands and rubbed them together as if he were a broker who'd just made millions. "Holy shit. I sure as hell don't see anybody wanting it now, do you?"

Stefan was ebullient, but I felt miserable. Another murder at SUM. It seemed unbelievable to me, and I could imagine the fed-up Michigan public and both houses of the state legislature storming the campus like the enraged villagers in *Frankenstein* and burning it to the ground.

"Maybe Sharon is right," I said. "Maybe there's some kind of curse to this place. I mean, jeez, we just saw Camille, we were just at her home, and now she's dead? Strangled? It doesn't seem possible."

The melodrama, the unreality of the situation, echoed inside of me: I was just a bibliographer, just an ordinary academic, yet here I was once again involved with a terrible crime.

"Wait," Stefan remembered. "Nina Bullerschmidt was there, too. She showed up after everyone else did, and I heard her saying something about wanting to have a late lunch in town with the dean and having called his secretary to find out where he was."

Sharon shook her head. "That's too elaborate. I bet she was already there and pretending to come to the scene late. After all, Nina's so meek, she'd be the last person you'd suspect of being a killer, and her ostentatious worship of Camille could have been a cover for hatred."

"Yes," I said. "Like Anne Baxter and Bette Davis."

"Little Miss Evil," Sharon brought out admiringly.

Stefan wondered if the surface couldn't have been the reality. "But what if Nina did actually adulate Camille, and Camille did or said something so horrible, so humiliating it drove her into a murderous rage?"

"Like?" I asked. "What could she have said or done that would be so terrible?"

Neither Stefan nor Sharon could suggest anything, and I wondered how I would get through the rest of the day with this new campus crisis. Would a sane person simply have packed his bags at that point and said living in a war zone was too much pressure? I had just read a thriller set during the mid-1990s siege of Sarajevo, in which a homicide cop stayed behind but sent his wife and daughter out of the city while it was still possible. He had a good reason to remain at his post. Did I?

But I was hooked on investigation, hooked on figuring things out, hooked on the drama. I asked Stefan if Coral was in the crowd gathered by Camille's office.

"She was, that's right. Why?"

"At the dean's reception, I heard Camille and Coral having some kind of argument and Camille talking about people being morons."

"That's typical of her. She looked down on everybody. They were probably just talking about critics of the endowed chair and her being chosen for it, that's all."

"The Board of Trustees should boot Littleterry and ask Stephen King to be president," I swore, and Sharon, who'd been studying Stefan, asked him if he was okay.

"Okay? I'm free! The Wicked Witch is dead! I won't have to look at her sour face at meetings, at parties, in the hallway, in the office, in the parking lot ever again. I don't have to think about people making fun of me for getting upstaged by that no-talent bitch."

At that moment, both our phones and the fax started ringing, and they didn't stop for the rest of the evening. The three of us watched the local TV news transfixed, alternately answering the phones or letting the machines take messages. There weren't more details than those Stefan supplied, but we taped the news anyway to watch it several times, like disaster junkies, or Princess Di devotees eating up tape of her funeral.

I was not proud of my response, but I found myself as much thrilled as shocked by what had happened. There was something obscene and primal about it, like slowing down on the highway to stare at the ambulance and wrecked cars in the median, a profound but not very admirable wallowing in the details, each one sending the message, "It's not you—you are alive."

We were all too wired to make dinner, so we ordered pizza and took out a Chianti Classico. But Sharon reminded us that it was Shabbat and that she was looking forward to lighting candles with us.

"And I brought you a treat." She went upstairs and returned with a CD, Ashkelon, and put it on. It was hypnotically melismatic Moroccan Jewish and Arabic singing by an Israeli cantor. That changed the mood completely, putting the necessary brakes on. We set the dining room table with the Belgian lace tablecloth my mother had given us and our good dishes.

When we lit the candles, we stood by them with Sharon between us, arms around each other, and chanted the blessing. With my eyes squeezed shut, I prayed silently for her to be safe and healed. Sharon sang the blessing over the wine in a softly pretty voice, and after we blessed the challah, I said, "You never used to be into Shabbat."

"Neither was Stefan, right? But when you get sick, things change. You're really focused on your body, intensely, but that also reminds you it's only a body, that there's a whole other level of existence. It's very strange. In New York I've started going to a really wonderful synagogue on the West Side. They sing a lot, and it's very warm. They have a meditation group, and I've even started doing Torah study."

"Really?"

She grinned. "I love it." I wanted to hear all about it and she was about to say more when the pizza arrived.

"This is a first," Stefan said. "We've never had pizza on Shabbat. I was ready to just skip it tonight, but—"

For a while, we talked about not having found a place for ourselves as Jews in Michiganapolis, how the synagogue seemed too stiff and formal, and that people's friendliness went no further than smiles. Warm ones, but that was it.

"See? You need to move back to New York. Living in Michiganapolis is Jewish exile."

"Move back and do what?" I asked.

"Open a detective agency," Sharon quipped. "I'll be your receptionist. And Stefan can follow you around for material."

He laughed. "Why does everyone keep saying I need material? I have too much to write about—and nobody to publish it." His eyes were suddenly heavy, and he rose to get another bottle of champagne to chill.

Clearly trying to deflect him from brooding about his career, Sharon brightly offered the theory that the harassment aimed at me (and perhaps partly at Stefan) was some kind of feint or red herring. So much for Shabbat, I guess.

As quietly jubilant now as if he'd won an award, Stefan said, "That makes a lot of sense."

I couldn't agree with them. "If someone at SUM wanted to set the stage for killing Camille, why target me or Stefan in any way, unless someone is trying to frame one of us for the murder?"

Sharon glared at me. "Either I'm drunk, or you're not making sense."

"Try both," Stefan said.

I explained that Valley had implied I was doing all the harassment myself.

Sharon snorted in disbelief. "If the point was turning attention away from Camille, it wasn't for long enough, or publicly enough, to make a difference, right? Since the killer got to her so soon after your office was broken into and your bibliography was scorched, it hasn't made the papers yet, because you haven't been blabbing about it."

Stefan had tuned out. Jauntily rubbing a second bottle of Bollinger in the ice bucket back and forth between his hands, he was oblivious. "How about an *Ab Fab* night?" he asked. "We could watch the episode where Edina falls out of the car."

I asked him if he had touched Camille's office door.

"Of course I did. And campus police are going to find my fingerprints in Camille's office, just like plenty of other people's, since everyone in EAR had been in and out of the former Jurevicius Library at one point or another. I don't think it was scrubbed clean after the books were ripped out and Camille moved herself and her major attitude in. So, kids, how about a party?" He was now practically giggling with delight.

"That's obscene," I said. "You can't celebrate her being dead."

"It would be a wake."

"You're not Irish."

Stefan chuckled. "But I like Enya."

"Stefan, you have to calm down. You can't be expressing so much satisfaction about Cypriani's murder; it'll make you a more appealing suspect and you'll get arrested for sure."

"Bullshit." Stefan bopped into the living room and switched the music to one of the sound-track CDs from 54, and disco was soon incongruously filling the house. Sharon grimaced, but I told her it was better than some of Stefan's other recent choices, like Iggy Pop's depressing *The Idiot*, which he listened to over and over. Or Schubert's *Die Winterreise*.

"That one's a real charmer," I griped. "The song cycle's about a man spurned in love who wanders off into the snow and goes mad and blind."

"Those merry Germans," she said.

"It got worse. He was into Gary Numan, too."

"Who's that?"

"That android-looking little guy from the seventies? Sort of Alvin and the Chipmunks in black satin shirt? Don't you remember him? Synthesizer pop—David Bowie without the sense of humor?"

"David Bowie had a sense of humor?" Sharon asked. "I'll have to rethink the seventies."

"You're not alone there."

"Come on, Nick, stop being so paranoid. Everybody hated Camille," Stefan said when he was back in the kitchen.

"But you're the one who she threatened the most, at least, that's how the campus police would see it. Valley's predisposed to dislike the both of us, and you'll make a great suspect, especially when you start setting off fireworks. Face it, you were the most important writer in EAR, but she came in like some cruise ship swamping a tugboat."

"Great image, babe." Stefan turned to Sharon: "See why I'm the writer and he's the bibliographer?" To both of us he argued, "Camille Cypriani's got to have been the least popular person in EAR in years, and that's saying a lot for a pretty hateful bunch of people."

"So why do you stay?" Sharon asked, and Stefan said he was living his dream. "I've been published, I've won prizes, I found a position as writer-in-residence. Sure, it's not what I expected, but what is in life?"

I stared at him, unable to believe his equanimity. This was the guy who a day ago could have been the main exhibit in a Misery Museum?

"It's not true that everyone hated Camille," I felt obliged to point out. "Nina Bullerschmidt *worshiped* her." I reminded them of what I'd seen at the reception, and Sharon, who herself had watched Nina and Camille at the so-called literary luncheon, suggested that there was something a little phony about Nina's adulation.

"Don't you think it seemed too public, like she wanted to make sure everyone saw her?"

"It's just the groupie mentality," Stefan demurred. "That's the whole point, that it's public, everyone watches you get some of that reflected glory."

And I added, "Look at all the Cypriani novels Nina had, right there in her home theater."

"Nina. Or the dean? What if the dean was the real fan, and Nina was somehow trying to undermine him, or Camille? Get to know her, get close to her, and then " Sharon shrugged. "And then do her dirt, somehow."

"*All About Eve*," Stefan said, and I smacked my hands together: "Yes! That's what crossed my mind at the party. Nina seems sweet and shy and downtrodden, but what if she's really a viper?"

Sharon made hissing noises, and we spent a few delirious moments recalling our favorite lines from that movie.

"Okay," I said. "What if Nina killed Camille because she was jealous of her, jealous that Bullerschmidt was so taken by Camille? Those could be *his* books in their home theater, not hers. And she was strangled, right? Isn't that the kind of thing a woman would be more likely to do than a man?"

Sharon pointed out that strangling took a lot of strength.

"Or surprise," Stefan said, and I noted the strong color in his face, his clear voice and eyes, his posture. Stefan wasn't just deeply contented, he was elated, overjoyed. Was Camille's death what it took to make him feel better? Shuddering, I thought of Updike's recent book where an elderly novelist took revenge on critics he hated by killing them.

Sharon opined, "In marriages where one person is publicly brutal and nasty and the other seems so much nicer, it's like the quieter one chose a mean spouse because he or she doesn't have permission to act that way. So they get profound satisfaction out of seeing the other partner do it all. Nina could be just as awful as her husband underneath the pearls and the prissiness. Or worse."

The doorbell rang, and Stefan warily went out to see if it was a reporter, but returned with Didier, who was drunk and angry, though still sober enough to acknowledge Sharon with a wave. "Man, I was just watching some asshole senators on TV and they kill me! Not an honest one in the bunch. Those fucking comb-overs and toupees that look like nasty pancakes. Who the hell do they think they're fooling? Am I supposed to take them seriously when they pretend to have hair? They're lying to the public, and they think we're stupid or blind or both." Didier smacked his attractive bald head, eyed the champagne, and asked for a glass, which Sharon smilingly poured him.

"Have you heard the news, Didier?" I asked. "No? Camille Cypriani was murdered in Parker Hall—well, she was found dead there."

Didier gaped at me. "Another body? *Tabernouche!* Can't you people grow up over there? Go into therapy, for Christ's sake!"

"*We* didn't do it," I said, and tried changing the subject by asking how Lucille was liking it down at Duke, where she'd been guest-teaching.

"Fine so far—nobody's been murdered there." Didier stalked off after downing his champagne with a cry of "God—you are all fucked."

13

S TEFAN said, "It's too bad Lucille isn't around to help calm Didier down."

"I miss her," I said, thinking that I really owed her a call.

"Well, at least Lucille's not a suspect," Sharon observed.

"Right? Because coming up from—where?—North Carolina, now that would be a long trip for harassment and murder, don't you think? Unless you were a real psycho and it didn't matter, or you wanted frequent flyer mileage."

The doorbell rang again, and this time it was Polly Flockhart, who came bustling in behind Stefan, looking very distressed.

"I heard the news about that Camille Cypriani endowed chair holder lady, and I left work early to see if you were all right. Do you need anything? Can I lend you some tapes I have on getting centered? Do you want a crystal for safety? I've got a good *feng shui* video that could help you create a more harmonious environment at home. Chimes? I have indoor and outdoor. Or I could let you take care of Maximilian for a day or two—that would give you a healing experience of unconditional love. Dogs can be so spiritual. No? You're sure?"

I did thank her, and accepted a hug before Stefan hustled her out. Sharon wryly asked who would be loving whom unconditionally—the dog or me and Stefan? "Is Polly for real?"

"She thinks she is. But she may just be a character Stefan invented. It's too soon to tell."

"I guess she means well."

Stefan grunted a soft "Hah."

I nodded. "Never say that; it's a terrible put-down whether you mean it that way or not. Samuel Butler wrote in *The Way of All Flesh*, 'If it were not such a terrible thing to say about a person, I should say that she meant well.' "

Sharon said, "Ouch. Well, whatever, you can for sure rule out Polly. I mean, she couldn't possibly have a reason to kill Camille."

"That's sometimes the person who did it in a mystery."

"Forget books, this is reality," Stefan snapped. "Can't you remember that?"

"Well, what's reality ever done for me?"

"But Didier," Sharon went on gracefully. "He's a grade-A USDA prime suspect. I mean, given Camille's fame and what all happened with his book. But I have to tell you, if one more person rings your doorbell tonight, I'll swear I'm in a *Seinfeld* rerun."

"How about some more pizza?" Stefan asked. We were tucking into second helpings when the doorbell rang, and we all started to laugh. Sharon almost dropped her pizza in her lap.

This time I got the door. It was Juno, looking drop-dead gorgeous in tight black jeans and a velvet leopard-print top under a black leather jacket.

"Have you figured out who killed Camille yet?"

She strode commandingly ahead of me to the kitchen, surveying the room as if expecting to see charts and maps and crime scene photos.

I protested, "It just happened."

Juno shrugged that off. "But you're quite the sleuth, Nick —what's taking so long?"

Sharon laughed, invited Juno to dinner, and we opened another bottle of Chianti. Stefan raised his glass to make a toast, and I expected him to praise Camille's killer, but he merely saluted the company, which at least seemed tasteful. Less couth was our discussion of what it would feel like to be strangled.

Stefan got drunker and kept threatening to do the Hustle and the Bump to the disco music that was still playing, while Sharon complained that she wanted to play something different. I suppose she missed the momentary peace of Shabbat we had briefly found before all the commotion of visitors.

Juno surveyed Stefan as he shook his broad shoulders and said, "Darling, I might join you if you get any looser."

I snuck out to the living room and, over Stefan's groans when the music stopped, put on M People's funky and romantic first album. When I returned to the raucous kitchen, Juno was wriggling her shoulders at the table to the beat of "One Night in Heaven," looking very inviting to me, and somehow being in the same room with her and Stefan did not seem then like a conflict, but rather a gift or a synthesis or a reunion.

I had to be smashed if it was making that much sense. And I avoided Sharon's knowing glance.

"I have a confession," Juno announced. "It's rather awful."

Well, that took the edge off for me, and we all sat up straighter.

"I have a secret. I have a book on the best-seller lists under a pseudonym."

We all goggled at her and issued various surprised comments and general noise. Was Juno the real Mitch Albom?

Drunk, wavering, defiant, pleased, giggly, Juno explained that she was "Victoria Vine," the author of *The Pharaoh's Last Stand*, an "Egyptian Western" in which the hero's name was Wy-att Earpotep. I had not read this massive book, which must have been three inches across the spine, only reviews that eviscerated it as "too dumb to be camp." The kindest had described it as equal parts *High Noon* and the cheesy 1950s *The Land of the Pharaohs,* with Jack Hawkins and Joan Collins.

"*You* wrote that crap?" Stefan roared, astonished. "*You* did?"

Juno nodded, delightedly bragging that none of her bad reviews affected sales in the slightest. "The book's being translated all over the world, even into Bulgarian," she laughed. "It's what pays for my clothes, the perfumes, my Lexus, everything delicious in life I could never afford on a professor's salary."

Stefan weaved over to where she stood leaning against a counter and crushed her in his arms. "Fucking A!" he yelled. "We have a winnah!" He picked her up and whirled her around, and I hoped he wasn't planning to audition for the Cirque de Soleil. When he set her down, she looked surprisingly flustered as she rearranged her clothes and patted her hair, and she eyed him speculatively.

Then she burst out, "I think my next venture should be a high-concept rewrite of Melville: what if Ahab was really a woman disguised as a man? I can call it Moby Pussy!"

Sharon shook her head.

I was amazed that Stefan enjoyed this revelation, that it didn't send him into the valley of professional death again, lamenting his own bad luck. His responding so exuberantly to Juno's success was a sign of how deeply relieved and released he felt because of Camille's murder—as if she had quickly come to symbolize everything that blocked and frustrated him.

Juno rattled on to Stefan about her trashy book, and I studied him, trying to figure out if his joy at Camille's death was normal and healthy, or if there was something perverse about it. Sharon took my hand across the table, squeezed it.

I remembered reading Virginia Woolf's diary entry about her rival Katherine Mansfield's dying, and how it pleased her. But Woolf was reflective and even embarrassed by her pleasure in Mansfield's death; she certainly didn't party hearty.

Last year when I discovered a body, I was anything but happy, and the vision still haunted me. Would Stefan escape that kind of lingering shock if he was so unperturbed now? All this was complicated by our dinner guest. Even though Juno stood right next to Stefan, her attractiveness wasn't dulled in the least; if anything, it was heightened. I wanted both of them, and if before that had felt soothing in some way, now it was confusing again.

The doorbell rang, and Sharon immediately started laughing so hard she almost slipped from her chair. "This is like a dorm!"

Stefan and Sharon were too engrossed in book talk, so I headed for the door, but it was a disappointment to open it to Detective Valley, who quietly seemed to sniff the air between us as if he had a built-in Breathalyzer. I didn't invite him in.

"Is Juno Dromgoole here?"

"Who wants to know?" Juno shouted from the kitchen. She surged down the hall and belligerently asked Valley what he wanted.

"I'd like you to come to the Campus Police Building at SUM to answer some questions about Camille Cypriani's death."

"Tonight? What for?"

"She was strangled with a leopard-print scarf, like the ones you reportedly wear."

"Who the fuck's been reporting *that*?" Valley pointedly regarded her top, and Juno rolled her eyes. "Okay, so I like leopard-print clothes. And?"

Stefan and Sharon were now clustered behind her, Stefan mockingly humming Darth Vader's theme from *Star Wars* until Sharon kicked him to make him stop.

Giving ground a little, Valley said, "Tomorrow morning at ten—or we'll send someone for you." He nodded goodnight to us, and I closed the door.

Juno blew up. "How the hell did he know I was here? I didn't leave a trail of bread crumbs. And I'm a Canadian citizen, he can't arrest me."

Sharon slipped an arm around her. "Valley just wants you for questioning, not an arrest. Maybe Valley thinks you saw something or know something that can help with the investigation."

"Does he think I'm a moron? I've watched your *Law & Order*—helping with the investigation is just an excuse to trap you."

Sharon turned off the stereo and sat with the complaining Juno in the living room while back in the kitchen, the mood sober, Stefan and I cleared the table and made coffee. Under my breath I asked, "Did you notice the scarf Camille was strangled with?"

"I wasn't looking at it," he whispered. "It was her face—But Juno did say she would strangle Camille if she were worth the effort," Stefan recalled sotto voce as we loaded the dishwasher. "At Bullerschmidt's reception, didn't she? I'm sure someone else heard her. Hell, how could anyone not have heard her?"

"Come on, that was just talk," I reasoned. But even as I said it, I began to think that Juno might have dropped by that evening for some reason connected to the murder, something I couldn't quite see. Maybe she did do it, and that question about whether we had figured out the murder wasn't just a joke. She might have been worried.

Unless she came by to see *me.*

Over coffee, out in the living room, the subject of Sharon's tumor came up.

"Acoustic neuroma?" Juno whooped. "My sister had one of those removed, just last year. Darling, it'll be worse than they tell you, much worse, but knowing that is going to be a godsend because you can't be disappointed and upset that you're not getting better fast enough. It will take ages to recover from the anesthesia alone. And never believe the doctors—it's the nurses who will tell you the truth. My sister was in the hospital three more times."

"Leakage?" Sharon asked unhappily.

"Yes. And you'll have to have private nursing to supplement what the hospital provides—there's simply no way they can give you the attention you'll need, and you'll need loads. But there's one thing you mustn't forget! They may be removing a tumor, but they're not cutting out your sense of style. Getting the right hairdo afterward will be crucial, but since you were a model, I'm sure you'll be fine."

Juno regaled Sharon with horror stories of her sister's surgery and hospital stay, but rather than tensing up more, Sharon seemed to relax about the whole situation, as did Stefan and I. Hearing Juno turn her sister's ordeal into a story somehow reduced the terror.

Juno gulped another cup of coffee before she left ("Marvel-ous"), and I nervously saw her to the door as if we'd had a date and I should be kissing her good-bye, Juno gave me a long full-body hug that left me shaken *and* stirred.

Back in the living room, Stefan was saying that he actually had come to like Juno a bit. "She's aggressive, but she's enter-taining, and she's a straight shooter in EAR where they lie more than congressmen."

I found myself unnerved by this admission and avoided looking at Sharon. One thing I did not want was Stefan and Juno getting to be pals—that would be even more awkward.

But later that night, Stefan and I had the wildest sex we'd had in weeks, and while Stefan slept, I contemplated the energy fueling it for each one of us: Stefan's joy that Camille was dead, my continuing attraction to Juno. Very murky.

In the morning, Stefan was up before me, and I found him in the kitchen with his arm around a weeping Sharon.

"He canceled," Stefan explained, as Sharon was unable to speak. "The surgeon at the Med School she was supposed to see for another consultation on Monday—he had to cancel her ap-pointment."

"Shit. Fuck."

"Right. And she won't be able to get in to see him until the end of next week."

Sharon pounded the table. "I felt like I had myself under control until today, but being rescheduled is too much to han-dle. Ever since I got my diagnosis, I've been feeling like I was plugged into a socket with too high a voltage, but I've been try-ing to stay calm. Now I just want to scream or break something, or—"

"Or kill someone?" I asked.

Sharon stared at me. "Yes!"

"Let's leave the paper outside," I said. "We don't need to see the headlines about Camille. Sharon, can I make you some French toast?"

"Like your Mom's?" she said hopefully.

"Exactly like hers."

She nodded, and blew her nose into a fistful of tissues. "I already had cereal, though. I'm kind of full."

"I don't care," I said, bossing her around like Cher cooking that steak for Nicholas Cage in *Moonstruck*. "You need some French toast—'for your blood'—and I need to make it."

She relented.

Stefan put up another pot of coffee, and I followed his movements, noting his jauntiness and ease despite Sharon's trauma. Even his voice was lighter, as if he'd been possessed and had an exorcism. I was glad, of course, but it was very disturbing; how long would it last? And how well would Stefan be able to keep from celebrating Camille's death publicly? Until the killer was found, he would be under suspicion, especially if he did nothing to conceal his satisfaction that she was dead.

"What if whoever killed Camille," Sharon said later over her heaped plate of French toast, "is someone with a brain tumor, or someone who's seriously ill, and finally snapped?"

Stefan sipped his Jamaica Blue Mountain, which Sharon had brought from New York. I told her we could get it in town, but she'd observed, "New York's a lot closer to Jamaica than Michigan is."

Answering her question, I said, "I thought stuff like that only happened on soap operas. Real soap operas. I mean, the fictional ones— Hell, I'm not sure *what* I mean anymore."

Stefan gently disagreed with Sharon. "I don't think whoever killed Camille had any medical trouble. You don't need that to hate her. Didn't," he corrected. "She was hateful enough all on her own."

"I think it's that weird guy," Sharon said.

Stefan and I both asked, "Which one?"

"The one in the basement of Parker Hall—the troll under the bridge."

"Which one?" I asked again.

"Cash. I know, I know. I said he was cute, but he's the obvious suspect—Camille took over his grandmother's library and desecrated her memory. Look at his tirade the other day."

It was certainly very possible, since of everyone in EAR,

Cash had the most personal reason for wanting to get rid of Camille Cypriani, and someone that angry and low in status could easily burst out in violence, Cash had been furious when he barked at us about Summerscale.

"If it's Cash, if he felt that way, why hasn't he killed Summerscale?"

"Maybe he's next," I suggested. "Maybe we should warn him. Maybe Cash is on a killing spree. He did say that Camille didn't deserve to live."

"But he mentioned Summerscale first," Sharon pointed out. "Remember?"

Stefan raised something else. "We have absolutely no idea how exactly Camille Cypriani got the endowed chair. We don't know how it was set up or by whom, and for what purpose. Everything's been hush-hush. And the same applies to President Littleterry's interest in White Studies. The man has the brains of Astroturf—he couldn't possibly have come up with a major curricular initiative on his own. So who's *really* behind it, and why? What if some sort of struggle is going on behind the scenes at SUM, and Camille's murder is connected to it?"

I jumped in. "Because she was just named chair of the task force, right? And then she's killed? So maybe she knew something and threatened someone. Jeez, paging Fox Mulder."

Sharon quoted Hercule Poirot: "Where there is murder, anything can happen."

We discussed what we knew about Cash Jurevicius, which wasn't much. He was single, supposedly brilliant, fluent in French, and deeply, deeply disappointed by the arc of his career. Like too many young scholars, he had left graduate school expecting to be part of the academic community just like the professors who had taught him, but he was merely a beggar at what passed these days for a feast.

I could tell that Sharon was enjoying all this speculation, that it took her mind off her illness and her canceled appointment.

"Didier's right," I said. "We *are* fucked. We have our annual department party, and our annual murder. How did I wind up teaching at a place like this, and how can it keep happening?"

Sharon had an answer. "SUM is a pressure cooker as bad as New York, only smaller and less honest. In New York people admit that it can be brutal and ugly, but here, you've got all this pretty scenery, and old buildings, and people talking about books—so it's actually worse when something terrible happens. It's more of a shock. If you were back in the city, this would barely make the front page."

Stefan disagreed. "Major writer—endowed chair? It's got money and celebrity. It's hot."

As if to confirm his analysis, the phone rang. When I grabbed it, a reporter from the *Detroit News* asked me what my relationship was with the deceased. "She was my twin sister, we were separated at birth!" I yelled, and hung up. Stefan and Sharon clinked forks on their plates in quiet congratulation.

"You'll say anything," Stefan marveled.

"Sometimes." I was prepared to say something even more outrageous when the phone rang again, and we all groaned. But it was Juno, fulminating about Detective Valley. "I went to answer questions without a lawyer because I had nothing to hide, but that shit-eating fake detective nailed me. He said witnesses at Dean Bullerschmidt's reception reported that I threatened to strangle Camille. They want to get rid of me!" she wailed. "Someone in this shithole department's trying to *frame* me —would I be idiotic enough to strangle that pretentious hag with my own scarf? But of course that kind of reasoning didn't carry any weight with Valley. He said I could have deliberately pointed to myself just to make that argument. He's insane!"

"Juno, you have to get a lawyer and contact the Canadian consulate in Detroit."

"Oh, I've already done that. It's all so revoltingly stupid. I was wearing Angel yesterday—does anyone think I could have been inconspicuous with *that* perfume on, sneaking into Camille's office and creeping back to mine? It's ludicrous!"

I agreed that she would have trouble being inconspicuous anywhere, and despite her rage, she cracked up. "Damned right."

When she hung up and I walked eager-faced Stefan and Sharon through her tirade, Sharon, who knew the Thierry Mugler perfume, said that Juno was absolutely correct. "Angel is very recognizable and very strong. But even without perfume, the idea of Juno carrying out a murder on the second floor of Parker without anyone noticing strikes me as absurd."

Stefan bought that completely. "But somebody did it, and sometime soon after Dulcie said Camille had gone down to her office. Somebody pretty clever. Or desperate."

"Don't start that conspiracy stuff again," I warned. "This is strictly personal, I'm sure of it."

Stefan shrugged. "Personal, and crazy. Somebody harasses you and me, then murders Camille, and tries to frame Juno? It doesn't add up." And he shook his head as if to indicate we should let it go; there were too many imponderables.

"So what happens now?" Sharon asked. "There's nothing we can do, no leads to follow up, and Angie isn't here. I bet she'd know what to do, she's been so smart and helpful before—"

I commiserated with Sharon, but said we had to try anyway.

"Wait!" Stefan interrupted. "You two are not getting involved in this. You are not investigating *any*thing." He pointed at Sharon: "You have a brain tumor. And you"—he pointed at me—"have a tenure review in process. Let Valley take care of it—it's his job."

I wouldn't back off. "But he's going after Juno—it's not fair. She thinks he's scum, and she told him that last year, remember? He's bound to hate her for that and want to get revenge. Don't you remember what it felt like being suspected of murder because he didn't like you?"

"Valley's rude, homophobic, and insensitive, sure—but that doesn't mean he'd railroad anyone."

"Yeah, right."

"But even if he wanted to, there's no way that we can help Juno. And why are you so concerned about her anyway?"

While I hesitated, Sharon saved me by saying, "Why *shouldn't* we be concerned? Juno's not a bad person, just a bit bombastic—"

"—*Boom*bastic is more like—"

"—and she has a good heart under all that glitz and noise. Besides, could you really stand by and watch her be persecuted?"

I chimed in: "Juno isn't stupid enough to strangle Camille with a leopard-print scarf, and she's not dedicated enough to kill Camille. She was angry at the party, but that's all. She flared up—it didn't mean anything. The people who are really angry, consistently angry, have been Summerscale and Cash Jurevicius. Both of them have a deep, abiding hatred for how they've been treated at SUM, and I can see either of them going after Camille. Summerscale because of what she represented, and Cash because of the insult to his grandmother."

"Was Grace Jurevicius really such a wonderful woman?" Sharon asked.

"All I know is that she's always been described as warm, loving, a gifted teacher and skilled, patient administrator. But that was before the university expanded like a cancer, and her values were trashed just like her library. God, you'd think the campus had been taken over by aliens, it's so different. And aliens into 'strategic planning'—what a way to conquer Earth."

Stefan returned us to Juno. "Nick, there's just no way that Juno could be convicted of murdering Camille if there isn't real evidence. Besides, what are you planning to do if you don't have a single lead? You can't go around interviewing everyone who might be a suspect, everyone who was there when her body was found—it'll enrage people and torpedo your tenure review. The dean? Serena? You can't ask them if they killed Camille. And Sharon can't do it for you—she'd have no excuse to make contact with those people."

"I could always call the medical examiner. She likes me, she's helped me before." But even as I offered that, I realized it was a pretty slim reed, given that I knew nothing much about the crime and that the ME certainly wasn't going to give me any more information than she wanted to. Though I would make the attempt anyway.

"So what's left?" Stefan mocked. "Bring all the suspects together like in a book and hope that the pot will simmer enough so that one of them cracks or gives something away?"

Sharon and I looked at each other. Then, in tandem, we said, "Exactly." And we high-fived each other.

"Not in this house! No way."

"Think of it as the party you wanted to have for Camille," I wheedled. "The wake, remember? It'll be just like Agatha Christie. We can even play Enya."

14

S TEFAN was as startled out of his anger as if I had slapped him. He grew quiet, and I could feel him being taken over by the idea, which of course was his in a way. "But how do you know one of those people at Camille's office did it—or that anyone would even come?"

Sharon said, "It's likely that someone in the crowd at Parker after Camille's body was found did it. Murdering her in such a public way, you'd have to want to see the aftermath, the reaction. To gloat. I know I would."

"And if the party or whatever is called in memory of Camille, no one we invited would dare stay away," I said. "We don't have to do much in the way of preparation. We have those hors d'oeuvres from Balducci's in the freezer," I mused. "We could time the thing for around cocktails tomorrow night. It's the weekend, people are free."

Ever practical, Stefan talked about the kind of invitations we'd make up on the computer, the kind of paper to get from Kinko's or Office Max, and how quickly we'd have to get them to people before Juno created some kind of international incident.

"That's right," Sharon said. "War with Canada can happen—look at the *South Park* movie."

"You watched that?"

Sharon nodded happily. "Twice. I even own a copy of *There's Something about Mary.*"

"*Girl*friend, what's up with that?" I asked. "Cultural slumming?"

"No. Facing brain surgery does things to your head."

"And your taste."

"Children—" Stefan said.

"Okay," I said. "Moving right along: I recommend a secret weapon. Essencia. It's a really potent dessert wine, and people will likely drink it like wine rather than a cordial. They won't know that it packs a wallop. It might loosen some tongues."

Sharon agreed. "I've noticed that the people at SUM I've met can't shut up when they have a few drinks—they're always saying something inappropriate."

I laughed. "That's a given here even without booze."

"Somebody is bound to drop something revealing under pressure, even if the pressure is simply from keeping the secret, right? Throw them all together and turn up the heat." Sharon practically rubbed her hands together and said, "Goodie."

"Wine. Our secret weapon is a dessert wine—" Stefan sighed, backing away from the general enthusiasm.

"It's either that, or we kidnap and torture them one by one," I said.

Sharon volunteered to do whatever shopping and setting up was necessary, and just call everyone to invite them, since it would be quicker. "I'll pretend that I'm Stefan's new personal assistant. I'll tell people it's a private memorial service for Camille, which will hit everyone right in their snob appeal."

Stefan wavered some more. "We're not in fifth grade, you know, planning a 'kewl' science project. This could be dangerous."

Sharon gave him a sly grin. "Parties always involve an element of risk—that's why they're so thrilling when they work. Look at Mrs. Dalloway's party! Forget the risk, Stefan, and think about the most important question, the one we haven't even considered."

He bit. "Which is—?"

"What do you wear when you're planning to unmask a murderer? At home."

Even Stefan laughed, and I said, "Instead of an endowed chair, SUM might want to see about securing enough additional funding to expand it to an endowed love seat. Maybe two people sharing the position could provide backup for each other."

While we cleaned up our breakfast plates, Sharon urged that we hold the cocktail party/investigation that very evening. "To surprise the killer." We agreed, and she said, "This is much more positive than talking about brain surgery. I'll be sorry when it's over. Unless it doesn't work, and you guys lose your jobs." We put together the guest list and Sharon made all the calls. No one declined.

I was absurdly happy after cleaning house with Sharon and Stefan, during which we talked solely of old times and new movies, avoiding the murder and the coming evening—not to mention Sharon's tumor. I was keenly aware of the artificiality of this mood. The whole phony memorial service idea might prove a fiasco, yet I felt satisfied to be doing something, facing my demons and helping out Juno, who I *knew* could not have killed Camille. I couldn't have told Stefan, but I was beginning to feel in tune with Juno, subtly connected in ways I didn't really understand. It was disquieting, it was fascinating. I was sure that whatever journey I was unexpectedly taking was far from over.

Straightening up by myself in my study later, I caught sight of my Wharton shelves, and suddenly something about the damaged bibliography in my campus office struck me and I went to the phone.

There was no sign the book was borrowed from the SUM or any other library, and I knew for a fact that the local bookstores didn't carry it, since it was specialized and expensive. I made some quick calls around town and learned that no one had put the bibliography on special order.

Okay, it was possible that the book had been ordered

on-line, but just in case that wasn't so, I called the academic publisher, whose staff I knew from experience was often in on Saturday mornings, and it didn't take long to find out what I wanted to know. The answer to who had bought and burned the book, and who had been harassing me, was something of a shock.

But I still wasn't sure how it connected to the murder, so I made a few more phone calls. When I was done, I realized that all along I should have been listening much more carefully to what people *said*, and connecting it to how the university functioned, and protected itself. Just to feel that I was finished, I called the ME and then dialed onto the SUM libraries system.

After lunch, Sharon and Stefan had laid an attractive spread of mixed hors d'oeuvres in the dining room with coffee, spring water, and Essencia on the sideboard, which Sharon had decorated with a bouquet of purple and white coneflowers. She and Stefan both looked great, and he seemed particularly delighted. He was wearing his Gaultier pants and shirt without the jacket, revealing his large, muscular arms. Sharon wore a lilac cashmere sweater and matching skirt: "I didn't think I'd get to dress up this much here!"

She and Stefan were so giddy they could almost have been decorating a Mardi Gras float. They didn't notice that I was a little distracted. I was pondering the incidents, the flyers, the books, the mailbox.

"We should do this more often," Stefan said several times, and Sharon sang out her agreement.

"Do what?" I asked. "Entertain murder suspects?"

Stung, neither one of them replied, and then the bell rang without the three of us having planned anything more than winging it. It could have been a children's book: *Nick and Stefan Solve a Crime.*

The Malatestas, Iris, Carter, Juno, and Serena arrived at the same time, as if they'd carpooled, and all our other guests appeared in the next fifteen minutes: Dulcie Halligan, Cash Jurevicius, Nina and Dean Bullerschmidt, Summerscale, Coral Greathouse. Everyone looked expectant and self-important.

People seemed gratified to have been invited but curious about the guest list, gazing around as if editing it.

The dean and Nina had never been to our house before, and Nina made brainless party guest comments, while the dean barely nodded. He seemed suspicious. Juno regaled the Malatestas and Cash with a recounting of her "confrontation" with Valley, making it sound as glamorous and daunting as a battle in *Star Wars*. Serena and Coral were locked in some low-voice conversation. Carter and Iris loitered in the kitchen with Stefan, asking if they could help and generally getting in the way. Dulcie had taken her wine into the sun room and was leafing through a gardening book while Summerscale sat out there, brooding, morose.

After everyone had a few glasses of wine, I called things to order in the living room and, as people drifted in, I thanked everyone for coming. They all clearly expected me to make a speech about Camille and perhaps to be asked to say a few words themselves. But instead, I announced, "I have a revelation about what's been going on in EAR."

The stillness in the room surprised me. From the wide range of guilty looks, there was apparently more going on than I had thought, but I plunged ahead, reporting on the last few days in which Stefan and I had been harassed. No one knew about all the incidents, and I was gratified by the show of disapproval, though Coral Greathouse and Dean Bullerschmidt looked annoyed that I was mentioning them in public—as if I had done something shameful. Unless they were afraid, as administrators, that I was planning legal action.

After talking about the burned copy of my bibliography, I turned to Cash Jurevicius and said, "I know you bought a copy of my book last week and had it overnighted to you, and I also know that you have no interest at all in Wharton. That wasn't hard to trace—you should have covered your tracks better. I called my publisher—I checked your publications at the library." I felt calm, triumphant, in control. Everyone was transfixed by this scene. "So why did you do it? Why did you torch our mailbox, break into my office, and burn the book? Why do any of it? What do you have against me, against us?"

"It's you," Cash said defiantly. "Just you. I wanted you to feel invaded. I wanted you to feel hurt, to feel what it's like when something of yours is destroyed, something you treasure. I know you love that bibliography, so that's what I wanted to destroy."

"The library," someone stage-whispered. "Grace's library."

"This is about the Memorial Library?" I asked. "But why target *me*?"

"Don't you remember what you said recently? You were in the hallway outside the EAR office, and you were joking about my grandmother's library. You said that her books would probably be burned at Homecoming. You couldn't resist mocking her, could you?"

"It was a joke!"

Cash stared me down, and abashed, I admitted it was tasteless, but I hadn't been making fun of Grace Jurevicius, I was making fun of—

I wanted to say EAR, the College of Arts and Letters, and SUM—but since my chair, my dean, and the provost were all in the room, it didn't seem like a path to career advancement.

"You can't joke about something like that," Cash told the whole room. "It's disgusting, it's obscene." Some people nodded, some looked away. Sharon was holding Stefan back; he was flushed and angry enough to pummel Cash. But I apologized to Cash, who looked as stunned as if he'd been coldcocked. He seemed so terribly wounded and beaten down just then, I couldn't manage to feel vindictive or angry.

"But you know what's really sad?" I said. "You complain about this department being coldhearted, and spitting on your grandmother's grave by acting the way it does, but you're not any better. You're worse—as Grace Jurevicius's grandson, you should be keeping her memory alive by how you behave, not just by worrying about her damned books."

Chastened, or maybe just pissed off, he turned away and sulked over by the fireplace.

"And do you know what's worse, Cash? You were so hurt by Camille's endowed chair and by how EAR wrecked your grandmother's library for it to give Camille an office, but I think we've all been hoodwinked." Cash turned and frowned. Then, addressing the entire gathering, I continued: "*I don't believe there is an endowed chair in EAR.* It's all been a hoax."

The room burst with questions and exclamations. Loudest was Stefan's, "What the hell are you talking about, Nick?"

I drank most of my wine, enjoying the spotlight, pausing dramatically before going on. "Put it all together. All everyone seems to talk about is the endowed chair, right? Ever since the summer. That's the first clue. It happened in the summer, when there are never lots of people around, and you can get away with—" I didn't finish the sentence, but everyone there knew that SUM traditionally pulled its fast ones ("academic innovations") over the summer, when the faculty bulletin and the student newspaper come out irregularly and news was easily muffled.

"There were some articles and an official press release. But it was anonymous? An *anonymous* endowed chair? That doesn't make sense. People always want their *names* associated with an endowed chair. That's the whole point—that's why you make the donation, so there's a professorship that will always have your name attached to it. But we were all so intrigued by wondering who donated the money, and so overwhelmed, that we never even considered the whole idea was ridiculous."

Puzzled looks in the room turned to comprehension, surprise, and some amusement.

"Even more suspicious," I continued, "is how it was funded. Right through the provost's office? That means no secretary in EAR would ever see a pay stub or a direct deposit slip if it was done that way. But why? Why keep it secret? The amount wasn't a secret, since all faculty salaries are public information. So why hide the checks—unless there *weren't* any checks in the first place, and that's what had to be kept a secret?"

I turned to Stefan, who gave me a thumbs-up, grinning his love and admiration for my perspicacity. "Remember what you said to me about the provost having power to do anything on campus?" Stefan nodded. "Well, only the provost could get away with something this bold."

All eyes turned to Coral, who kept her head up, face frozen. "Camille was always so controlled, always aloof," I said, "Wasn't she? Mean, but quietly mean. She never let much out. Except once, when Cash called her a fraud at the literary luncheon. Why? Why would that one word push her buttons unless she was faking something big? And why did she say to Coral at the dean's reception that people were morons, that they believed whatever you told them, whatever they saw? Coral must have been anxious about the scam. We were all so dazzled by the announcement of the chair, and so put off by her personality, that we didn't look at it closely. The money, the PR, and Camille's Pulitzer all fooled us."

"Camille's bluster," Juno said. Then she asked, "Why would anyone bother with such an elaborate charade?"

"I don't know, but my guess is that it was all for PR. SUM benefited from Cypriani's reputation, and she got a berth that put her in a much higher class of novelist at a time when there's increasing competition for a spot on the best-seller lists." Watching Nina's deep blush, I suddenly asked her, "Was it *your* idea?"

Terrified, Nina stuttered out, "I wrote a fan letter to Camille saying I wished, oh I wished she were teaching at SUM. She was so inspiring! So noble! So generous!"

At that moment, I couldn't help thinking of a line on Bette Midler's debut album, "Oh, honey, she is twisted." And Nina seemed as pathetic, lost, and friendless as Julie Harris in her opening scenes of *The Haunting*.

"That's what must have set the whole thing in motion," Nina brought out, head down. "But I thought it was real! Nobody told me it was a fake," she whined, and the dean lay an admonishing hand on her arm to shut her up. He turned to Coral and asked, "There was never an endowed chair? You made that up between you, you and Camille?"

Coral, as impassive as ever, didn't deny it, didn't confirm it.

The Malatestas were chuckling, but stopped when Juno asked why Camille was murdered. What did that have to do with the chair being fraudulent?

I had an explanation. "At first I thought the harassment I

was receiving was connected to Camille's murder in some way, but now I see that the leopard-print scarf Camille was strangled with meant that whoever killed her hated her, and also hated Juno enough to want to frame *her* for the crime. I called the medical examiner to ask about that scarf, and they had traced it. It's from Target."

Juno laughed scornfully.

I felt clearheaded and in command as it all began fitting together.

"A designer scarf, yes—a scarf from Target, no. Not for Juno. My cousin Sharon said that people in EAR talk a lot, so I searched my memory, trying to think of who I'd heard saying hateful things about Camille *and* Juno. The vitriol had to be directed at both of them." Then I turned to Iris, who I noticed had been slowly backing out of the room, but stopped when our eyes meet. Before I could say anything at all, she screamed, "Carter did it! It was his idea!" Carter lunged at her, calling her a lying bitch. They kicked and cursed while Stefan and Bill Malatesta rushed over to hold them apart and keep them from hurting each other or anyone else. In all the commotion, I was surprised nothing got knocked over or broken, but then they were a diminutive pair, for evildoers.

"It worked," I thought. "It really worked."

Sharon slipped into the kitchen to make a call, and in a very few minutes Valley and one of his officers were leading Iris and Carter off while they demanded lawyers.

The party broke up almost immediately, with Coral Greathouse making the fastest exit, followed by the dean, who seemed to be in lumbering pursuit. Nina wrung her hands like a silent screen heroine and made a teary apology to the whole room before entering his wake. When she left, Serena told me that with Iris and Carter under suspicion of murder, my tenure review committee would have to be totally reconstituted. "There may be some serious delays," she said grimly.

Cash approached me. "I'll pay for the new mailbox, and any other damages I've caused. But please don't press charges. I've disgraced my family's name enough."

Feeling generous and sympathetic—and that all things considered, I'd had a lovely evening—I assured him I wouldn't.

Juno was the last to leave. I walked her to the door, where she kissed me full on the lips, and I was glad we weren't in each other's arms because I would not have wanted to let her go. "You like to ferret things out, don't you? Dig and delve?" she asked, looking as hungry and dangerous as Sandra Bernhard circling Jerry Lewis in *The King of Comedy*. As I saw her out, I remembered "Everything will burn!"

Maybe Sharon was right. If I needed at my age to find experience with a woman, Juno might simply be out of my league. Or maybe I wanted to play with fire. As I turned from the door, I thought of Juno as a character George Eliot had described in *Middlemarch*: "a bright creature, abundant in uncertain promises."

With guests gone, we sank onto the couch, exhausted and amazed.

"Some party," Sharon said, "though I thought you'd drag it out longer and confront each person one by one like in *Murder on the Orient Express*."

"That would have taken too long."

Sharon praised me for figuring out as much as I had.

"Well, I should have seen it more clearly, figured out sooner who was behind the harassment. Stefan always warns me that I should be careful about what I say in public, and making that joke about the Jurevicius Library books being burned at Homecoming was a big mistake. People thought it was funny, people repeated it like I was fucking Voltaire or something, and it made Cash mad. So what he did to get back at me made sense as a response; it had a theme: flames, fire, hellfire. It was kind of elegant, in a way."

Appalled, Stefan said, "It was nuts, and it was criminal. It scared the shit out of you and depressed both of us."

"Cash is just a victim of a screwed-up system."

"That would make a great argument in court," Stefan threw off, unconvinced.

"No, I can see that it was very human." I felt quite reflective and forgiving. Then I quoted Henry James's advice to a young writer: "Try to be someone on whom nothing is lost." And I added, "But the so-called endowed chair was obvious, hidden in plain sight. It was splashy enough to hide the lies, and once I started putting the pieces together, well—"

I felt momentarily satisfied and accomplished. Then I started to experience the inevitable crash after the high, and that instantly retriggered my doubts and anxieties about what had happened to my life in the last few years.

"It's like Bangladesh," I said.

"What?" Sharon was puzzled. "The country or the concert?"

"You know how meteorologists talk about Bangladesh being in Cyclone Alley, how hurricanes just sweep in there, with huge floods, thousands of people die? Half the country's underwater for weeks, people starve, they get cholera or typhus because there isn't any clean water. Then it's over, and everybody rebuilds, and they go on until the next one. We're not moving from here, we can't. It's a wonderful place to live, a pretty Bangladesh. We have our own little cyclone, our own destruction that seems to smack us down almost every year. I don't know why it's turned out that way, but it has."

"Isn't that an exaggeration?"

"Yes, and no."

Sharon reminded me that my life may have some terrible disruptions—"But they *are* disruptions. They're not the main theme."

"This is not a normal life. I mean, if I were taking one of those magazine stress tests, I'd be way off the chart. They ask you about divorce and work and being overweight, but they never say, 'Have colleagues of yours recently been murdered?' "

"Okay, okay—but you're blessed because you're not alone. You have Stefan."

"True enough. But wasn't it yesterday you were telling me that my life was a mess, and Stefan and I needed to get out of here?"

"That was before you solved another crime."

"Two crimes," I corrected.

Then I told them that Ross Macdonald had said the great appeal of mystery novels was in their "symbolic attempt to grapple with the American fear of death, for which our culture makes such meager provision, and to fit it into life." I speculated, "So maybe teaching the new mystery course in the spring will help me deal with the last few years of turmoil, one way or another."

Stefan wasn't completely attentive; he seemed to be piecing things together for himself aloud. "If Camille pulled such a wild stunt, she must have been under amazingly fierce pressure to revive her career. I bet her sales were slipping, though I don't get it. She has her face on a Barnes & Noble mug. She's at the top, or close to it, for a quasi-literary writer." He seemed puzzled, but replete.

I let him chew on it, hoping that perhaps he'd feel less terrible about his own blighted career.

"Nick, are you going to get in trouble for tonight?" Sharon wanted to know. "Because they can't hush this up, can they? And won't Coral have to resign? Won't there be a scandal?"

Stefan chuckled. "I think Nick is truly safe. He's a whistle-blower, he exposed a fraud. SUM will have to thank him. And they'll have to give him tenure, or it'll look like persecution and make for a nasty news story and an even nastier potential lawsuit. PR rules at SUM, now and forever."

We considered that terrain of threats and promises. I thought of tenure at SUM. Being trapped in EAR for decades.

Sharon still had questions. "How could Iris and Carter have done it, have killed Camille? I mean, not emotionally, but technically?"

I didn't find it hard to picture the scene: "They were in her beautiful big office, sucking up to her in some *All About Eve* kind of way, just like I saw them try to do at the dean's reception right after they tore her to shreds for me. So—Camille was sitting at her desk like the owner of a manor granting an audience to her starving tenants. One of them slipped behind her, made some kind of a comment about the wonderful view, and took out the scarf—At least that's how I would have done it with Stefan."

"Then who was Little Miss Evil?"

"There's more than one candidate. Besides, it's more a gestalt than an identity."

"Oh." Sharon looked unimpressed.

The phone shrilled, and Stefan said, "More reporters," but headed to the kitchen, where we heard him say a glum hello to his agent. I braced for the worst, and expected I was right when Stefan bellowed, "*What?*" But then I had no idea what could be going on when Stefan's next question was, "Keanu Reeves? You're kidding!"

Sharon and I rushed to the kitchen, where Stefan was saying, "Fine—I'll wait for your fax." He hung up and ordered us both to sit down. We obeyed. Eyes wide, Stefan announced that Keanu Reeves had found a copy of Stefan's out-of-print first novel in a used bookstore, and his production company was negotiating for the screen rights.

"It's sure to be a six-figure deal! And if the film ever gets made, we could be rich. And they want *me* to write the screenplay!"

"Keanu Reeves buys books?" I asked. "Used books? And reads them?"

"If it's a hit," Sharon raved, "you can leave this nuthouse and go to Hollywood. God, what am I saying? That's just what you need! You should stay here and hire some bodyguards. Hunky ones. One for each of us."

Stefan sat down, as winded as if he'd just finished a marathon.

I reached over, cupped his chin in my hand, and looked him in the eyes. "Wait a minute, Stefan. Didn't you tell him that you weren't interested, that you were giving up writing as a career? And if you were going to sell your book, it would only be possible if Jean-Claude Van Damme played the lead?"

EPILOGUE

SHARON had her surgery three weeks later at the best hospital in Michiganapolis, and sitting in the truculently cheerful waiting room the day of her operation, I kept thinking that I wasn't ready, wasn't ready to lose her or even face the possibility of it. The room tried its best to soothe all fears with its baby palette of pink and blue, its framed reproductions of Renoir. But the vibrant music of French merriment seemed strikingly inappropriate to me.

"The chairs are comfortable," Sharon's father said with stolid approval. He was right to appreciate them, since we sat there in shifts for over fifteen hours, though the surgery was supposed to take only eight.

"It's like home remodeling," I said early into the afternoon when we were starting to panic. "The estimates are always wrong."

"Nick, dear," Sharon's mother said under her breath. "I know you're trying to help. Please shut up."

So I did. We read, did crossword puzzles, stretched, retrieved tasteless plastic-wrapped food from the cafeteria, while I studied the elderly, round-faced, chubby little couple who had always seemed such unlikely parents for a daughter who would become a model. They'd marveled quietly themselves at the disparity for years, eyeing her with constant appreciation the way a short father admires his tall, basketball-playing son. "I did good," he might think, as proud as an artist, a sculptor, an architect, for what he's put into the world, his legacy, his gift.

I watched other families and friends, some dazed, some hopeless, some with faces clawed by the pain of not knowing—or of knowing too much.

Stefan read student manuscripts. I graded papers. Or tried. I drank gallons of bad coffee and for each cup tried to drink as much bottled water, so that I was constantly heading to and from the nearby men's room, which had far too many mirrors in which you could see what grief looked like.

Everything about the hospital repelled me, from the smell to the busy staff to the weak patients, some being wheeled around corners and some in robes taking halting hallway walks with their IV bottles on rolling stands. I had not been prepared for this assault, this memento mori clamor. Or the occasional code-blue alerts that sent staffers pounding off like frantic troops.

I remembered Sharon's drowsy last words: "I'll see you on the other side." She was right to think of the surgery as a dividing line, a marker. Unless she meant something more permanent. Like many desperate and frightened people, I made crazy bargains with whomever or whatever force out there might agree to take me up on them.

I had to swat away lines from books that kept pestering me, because they were all so grim, like Kate Croy in *The Wings of the Dove* intoning, "We shall never again be as we were."

I slept on and off. I cried, quietly, sitting on a closed toilet, the stall locked.

While the neurosurgeon was chipping away at her seventh nerve to get every bit of the tumor, we received periodic updates from gentle-voiced nurses. The surgery was proving more difficult than expected because there were some anomalies in

Sharon's cranial structure, and one artery wasn't exactly in the right place. Stefan and her parents discussed all the technical aspects of the surgery with the avidity of antique car collectors at a road rally. I tuned them out, disgusted to think of someone, something, inside Sharon's head, to think of her as parts and not herself. The word *microsurgery* gave me no comfort.

I called my parents in New York to give them my own updates. And I cried some more, tentatively, as if trying to assess the depth of my sorrow and fear. I could have been someone walking around a crater, not comprehending at first its size and depth, but walking, measuring, surveying, growing slowly and painfully aware that it was enormous, frightened by its magnitude, its threat.

This felt like a disaster, not a rescue.

The blond, blue-eyed neurosurgeon emerged at the end, reeking, pale, and sweaty, but as triumphant as a SWAT team captain who'd gunned down a terrorist. "We got it all," he said, and unlike her parents and even Stefan, I did not feel grateful. If anything, I wanted to scream at him for misjudging the length of the surgery and underestimating, for even doing it at all. Why couldn't he have suggested an alternative? I hated him, I hated life.

They let her parents see her that evening.

Stefan and I drove down to the hospital the first thing in the morning after a drugged and ugly sleep that left me feeling leaden. I actually dreaded seeing Sharon, not having ever visited someone so ill, and leaving the elevator, heading down the bustling cold hallway, was painful.

The teddy-bearish black nurse Sharon's parents had hired met us at the door, expecting us. After she said hello, Stefan asked, "*Vous êtes Haitienne?*" Tuned into accents, even then.

"*Vous pouvez entrer, monsieur,*" she whispered to me, assuming her native language would comfort me, I suppose. I left them chatting quietly at the door about Sharon's condition, and tiptoed into the small, barren private room, which seemed to gobble the color and fragrance of the flowers we had sent. I had a vague, nauseating sense of machines and tubes and heavy bandages smothering Sharon like the snakes enwrapping Laocoön. Why was everything so white, including her?

Sharon's eyes seemed unfocused. And she looked so tiny, as if the whole hospital had her in its grip now. I sat by her bed and touched her free hand, brought it slowly to my lips.

"Sweetie, I feel like I'm underwater. I must look terrible," she murmured, the woozy words drawn out and slow, just on the edge of clarity. I'd been warned by her parents that she would be hard to understand, but I had no trouble. She sounded as if her mouth and tongue were merely numb after a root canal.

I felt locked on her eyes as if I were an exhausted mariner lost at sea finally sighting land on the horizon: no longer beleaguered, but humbled by relief.

"I've never seen you looking more beautiful," I said, and Sharon gave me a tiny, crooked smile from the unparalyzed, unbandaged side of her face, because she knew that I meant it.